MY BOOK OF
OLD-TIME FAIRY TALES

BEAUTY AND THE BEAST

MY BOOK OF
OLD-TIME
FAIRY TALES

ILLUSTRATIONS BY
MARGARET EVANS PRICE

BARNES
&NOBLE
BOOKS
NEW YORK

This edition published by Barnes & Noble, Inc. by arrangement with
Checkerboard Press, Inc.

1995 Barnes & Noble Books

ISBN 1-56619-765-1

Printed and bound in Hong Kong

M 9 8 7 6 5 4 3 2 1

CONTENTS

INTRODUCTION

My Book of Old-Time Fairy Tales invites readers into a magical world filled with heroes and heroines, elves and fairies, princes and ogres. These seventeen stories, lavishly illustrated by Margaret Evans Price, will delight both children and adults.

In the days of "once upon a time when pigs spoke of rhyme" most of the stories in this book were already well known. We do not know who created them, but we are sure that children chuckled over the surprising adventures in them, as they have continued to do so for generations. We may also safely guess that the older folks who told these stories got just as much fun out of them as the younger folks who listened. Good storytellers had fun trying to improve the stories as they told them by adding a twist to the plot or a new turn of words here and there. Then, when they were pleased with their changes, they retained them in future tellings. For you must remember that for a long, long time these stories were not written down in books, but were passed along through oral tradition.

My Book of Old-Time Fairy Tales is rich in truths of the imagination. Children will delight in seeing a pumpkin transformed into the gilded coach that carries the fair Cinderella to the grand and glorious ball where she meets her Prince. Their imaginations will soar when told of the story of Rumple-stilt-skin, the elf made of gingerbread, who dances for joy at the thought of his secret knowledge. Everyone will be captivated by the adventurous tale of brave Hop o' my Thumb, who leads his six brothers out of the dark forest, but only after fighting and defeating the evil Ogre. And, let us not forget the silly story of the Old Woman who desperately searches for the thread that will free her pig so she can reach home before dark!

My Book of Old-Time Fairy Tales is an inspiring volume that will quicken your pulse and make your heart beat faster. Breathtaking and splendorous adventures await you!

KING HAWKSBEAK

Once upon a time there was an old King who had only one daughter. He was very anxious that his daughter should marry, but while she was more beautiful than words can tell, she was so proud and rude that no man who came to woo her was good enough for her. She sent away one after another and even made fun of them to their faces.

One day her father gave a great feast and invited to it all the young bachelors of royal or noble blood from far and near. After the feast they were all lined up in a row according to their rank—first kings, then princes, then dukes, earls, and barons. The Princess was led down the line and told to choose a husband, but she carried her head high and found something wrong with every one.

The first was too fat. "You're too chubby, too round and tubby," she sneered. The next was too tall. "Long and lean, close and mean!" The third was too short. "Stout and short, not my sort!" The fourth was too pale. "What a gawk! White as chalk!" The fifth, who kissed the hem of her dress, was too red. "Don't peck my frock, you turkey-cock!" The sixth was not straight enough to suit her. "Why should

1

THE PRINCESS AND THE RAGGED BALLAD-SINGER

I pick a crooked stick?" So she went down the line making her saucy rimes. But she saved her choicest mockery for one young king who was the wonder of the world for beauty and strength, but whose nose was the least bit hooked. He would have asked her to be his queen, but she brushed rudely by him with the rime:

"Why should I stay for the silly talk
Of one whose nose is the beak of a
hawk?"

After that he was always called King Hawksbeak.

When the old King saw that his daughter only made fun of all her fine suitors, he was very angry. "By my beard," he swore, "the first beggar who comes to the door shall be her husband!"

Only a few days later a strolling ballad-singer took his stand under one of the castle windows and sang his best in hope of alms. When the King heard him, he said: "Let the fellow come up here." So the beggar was brought in, ragged, stooping, with wild hair, and whiskers that almost hid his face. He sang to the King and the Princess all the ballads he knew and then held out his torn hat for coppers, or perhaps a bit of silver.

The King said: "Your song has pleased me so much that I will give

you instead of money this daughter of mine for your wife."

The Princess cried out in disgust and dismay. But the King said: "I have sworn by my beard that you, too proud for royal suitors, should marry the first beggar who came to the door. That oath cannot be broken."

This king could be very stern when he chose, and the tears of his daughter did not move him. The court chaplain was called in and the Princess and the beggar were married then and there.

And then, although his daughter clung to his knees, the King shook her off. "Now you are a beggar-woman, and beggar-women do not live in palaces. Go hence with your husband."

The ballad-singer took his bride by the hand and led her out of the castle; she who had never before set sandal to the ground had to go with him on foot.

They came to a beautiful, leafy wood, and the Princess asked:

"Who is the lord of this forest so
    fine?"
"It belongs to King Hawksbeak.
    It might have been thine."

"Oh, I was a proud and foolish
    young thing.
 I would I had wedded that glori-
    ous King."

Soon afterward they reached a wide meadow, and she asked again:

"Who is the lord of these meadows
    so wide?"
"They belong to King Hawksbeak,
    who sought you for bride."

"Oh, I was a proud and foolish
    young thing.
 I would I had wedded that glori-
    ous King."

Then they passed through a large town, and again she asked:

"Who owns this city so thronging
    with life?"
"It belongs to King Hawksbeak,
    who wished you for wife."

"Oh, I was a proud and foolish
    young thing.
 I would I had wedded that glori-
    ous King."

"Enough of this!" exclaimed the beggar. "Why should you be wanting another husband? Am I not good enough for you?"

But the poor Princess, who had been so sharp of tongue, said never a word. She did not speak again until they came to a miserable hovel, when she cried out:

"This wretched hut, this cabin, to
    be mine!
 He's better housed who feeds my
    father's swine!"

The begger answered: "This is my house and yours. Here we are to live together and I hope you'll be content."

The door was so low that she had to bend her haughty head to enter. All was dark and empty within.

"Where are the servants?" she asked.

"Servants, indeed!" laughed the beggar. "Do you forget whose wife you are? If you want anything done, do it yourself. Light the fire and put the kettle on to get my supper. I am hungry."

But the Princess knew nothing about lighting fires or even putting on the kettle, and so to have any supper the ballad-singer had to do the work with his own hands, that were not so very skillful about it, either.

It did not take long to eat the black bread and cabbage soup which was all they had for supper. The bed was of straw, with a log of wood for a pillow, but the Princess was so tired she slept soundly, and was by no means ready to waken when the beggar made her get up. All day long he kept her busy scrubbing the poor house.

They lived like this for a few days, until their bread and cabbages were all gone.

Then the beggar said: "Wife, this won't do any longer; we can't live here without working. You shall make baskets."

So he went out and cut some rushes, and dumped them down before her. The Princess began to weave them as best she could, but

the stiff rushes bruised her tender hands.

"You cannot weave," said the beggar in a tone of disgust. "You would much better spin; any woman can do that."

Then the poor Princess sat down at the broken old wheel and tried to spin, but the harsh yarn cut her delicate fingers and made them bleed.

"Now," said the beggar angrily, "you see what a good-for-nothing you are. I have made a bad bargain in you. But sitting in the market place will not be too difficult even for you. I will get some crockery and you shall offer it for sale."

"Alas! how can I do that?" thought the unhappy Princess. If those before whom I have held my head so high should come and see me sitting in the market place offering pots for sale, it would be their turn to scoff." But she dared not disobey her husband, for fear he would leave her to die of hunger.

Her first day in the market place was not so bad. The people willingly bought of her because she was so beautiful, and they paid what she asked for her wares—nay, some even gave her the money and left her the pots as well.

She and the ballad-singer, who did nothing but sit on the doorstep

in the sun, lived on the gains as long as they lasted, and then the beggar laid in a new stock of cups and plates and pots and jars. The Princess took her seat at the entrance of the market and began to cry her wares in a low voice. But before she had sold a thing, a soldier on horseback came galloping up and rode right over her crockery. Crash! Crash! Cups and plates and pots and jars were broken into a thousand bits.

The Princess began to cry, and was so dismayed that she stopped only to pick up the two unbroken pots. "What will my husband say to me?" she cried. Home she ran, and with tears and trembling she told her story.

"Stupid! Who would ever think of sitting at the entrance of the market with crockery?" he said. "Stop that crying. I see you are no manner of use for any decent kind of work. I have been to our King's palace and asked if they do not want a kitchen drudge, and they promised to try you. You will get scraps enough to feed us both, at any rate."

So the Princess became kitchen drudge in King Hawksbeak's palace, and she had to wait upon the cook and do all the dirty work. At her husband's bidding she hung from her waist, one at each side, their two unbroken pots, and in

them took home all the scraps and leavings. On these they lived, and many a crust and many a rind did the Princess gnaw which she would scarcely have thrown to a dog in the days of her pride.

One morning she heard that the sister of the young King was to be married that evening. The cook made her stay late to help, but at last gave her a few moments of freedom, and she dragged herself upstairs and stood behind a door to peep at all the splendor.

When the rooms were lighted with their thousands of candles, and she saw the guests streaming in, each one more beautiful than the last, she thought with heavy heart of her sad lot, but she blamed only herself for the pride and rudeness which had lost her such happiness and brought her to such trouble.

Now and then the upper servants, as they passed, threw her bits from the savory dishes they were carrying away from the feast, and these she put into her pots to take home.

All at once, just as the dancing began, a splendid lord came in. He was dressed in silk and velvet, and wore a gold chain about his neck. He spied the beautiful woman who was hiding behind the door, seized her by the hand and, though making a wry face at her shabby gown, asked her to dance with him.

The Princess shrank back and shook her head. Her first glance told her it was King Hawksbeak, who had been one of her suitors and whom she had driven away with scorn and insult. But kings are used to having their own way. He laughed and drew her out into the middle of the ballroom. The string by which the pots were suspended at her sides broke; down fell the pots, shattered to pieces, and the chicken bones and edges of pie crust were spilled all over the ballroom floor.

When the guests saw this they burst into shouts of mocking mirth. The Princess was so ashamed she would gladly have sunk into the earth. Through the door and down the stairs she dashed, but running feet came after her and a strong arm held her fast. When she looked at her captor, she saw it was King Hawksbeak.

He spoke to her tenderly and said: "Do not be afraid of me. My hair is cut and my whiskers are gone. I am King Hawksbeak. I was the beggar who married you. I was also the soldier who rode over your crockery. For love of you have I done these things that your beauty might be made perfect by sympathy and gentleness. Forgive me, my Queen, for all I have let you suffer."

She wept bitterly and said: "I was very wicked, and I am not worthy to be your wife."

But he answered: "Be happy! Those evil days are over,—all left behind us with our broken pots. Now we will celebrate our true wedding."

Then came the waiting-women, who clad her in bridal raiment, and her father with all his court rode through the palace gate and wished her joy on her marriage with King Hawksbeak. Her father never told her whether he knew who the ballad-singer was. Did he?

THE DANCING SHOES

There was once a King who had twelve daughters, each more beautiful than the one next younger, so that the eldest was most beautiful of all. They slept in one chamber where their beds stood side by side, and every night when they were well tucked in, the King locked and bolted the door. But when he unlocked the door in the morning he saw that their satin shoes had been danced to shreds, and no one could find out how that had come about, not even the royal schoolmaster, who was the wisest man in the world.

Then the King bade the heralds proclaim that he who could discover where and with whom the princesses danced at night, should choose one of them for his bride, but that whosoever dared to make the venture and failed to succeed within three nights should lose his liberty.

It was not long before a Prince came riding to the court and offered to make the trial. He was received and feasted with all honor, and in the evening was led into a room next to the great chamber where the princesses all slept. A bed was made ready for him beside a little window in the wall between the rooms, but he was warned not to sleep. He was to watch and see

9

after this and undertook to solve the puzzle, but all fell asleep too soon and had to vanish.

Now it chanced that a poor Soldier who had been wounded and could serve his king and country no longer, found himself on the road that led to the city where the King lived. There he met an old dame, who asked him whither he was bound. "I hardly know myself," said he, and added in jest: "I had thought of trying my luck at finding out where the princesses dance their satin shoes to shreds."

"Try, brave Soldier," said the old dame, who was a fairy in disguise, "but mind you do not drink the wine that will be brought to you at night, even though it be offered by the hand of the eldest and most beautiful princess." With that she gave him a short green cloak embroidered with fern seed, and said: "When you wear this, you will be invisible, but you must be careful to tread as silently as a shadow." So the Soldier took heart, went to the King, and announced himself as a suitor. He was honored for his wounds and feasted as well as the princes.

That evening at bedtime he was led into the antechamber where the eldest princess graciously offered him a goblet of wine through the

where they went and danced, just as their nurse used to watch them through the window that, though small, was large enough to let her go in to them when they were ill or naughty.

But the eyelids of the Prince grew heavy with sleep, for he had traveled far and feasted well. Soon he sank into a deep slumber, and when he awoke in the morning, beside each empty bed stood a pair of white satin shoes with the soles danced into holes. On the second and third nights it happened just as before, and the poor Prince was given over to the court wizard, who had only to wave his ivory wand over a man and at once that man vanished like a puff of smoke. Other princes came

THE PRINCESS OFFERED THE SOLDIER A GOBLET OF WINE

youngest said: "I know not how it is. You are all gay, but I feel frightened; some danger is whispering to my heart."

"Little goose, thou art ever frightened," said the eldest. "I, for one, never felt so glad before. Hast thou forgotten how many kings' sons have already tried in vain? What harm can come to us from this poor Soldier, so tired that he hardly needed the wine with its juice of sleepy poppy?"

When they were all dressed for the ball, each of the twelve princesses slipped her head through the little window for a look at the Soldier. He seemed fast asleep, so they felt quite secure. The eldest went to her bed and tapped it; it instantly sank through the floor, and one princess after the other sprang through the opening, the eldest going first.

The Soldier, who had watched everything from under his eyelashes, did not tarry longer, but threw on the fern-seed cloak, slipped through the window, and went down last. The twelve princesses were descending by a marble stair into the heart of the earth. Halfway down the Soldier trod on the long silk train of the youngest; she was terrified and cried out: "What is that? Some one is pulling at my dress."

"Don't be so foolish!" called back the eldest. "Did no train ever catch

window. He took the goblet with all courtesy from her hand, but he had tied a sponge under his chin, and so let the wine run down into it without drinking a drop. Then he fell upon his bed beside the little window and after a few minutes began to snore like a trumpet. The twelve princesses in the next room laughed to hear him, but the eldest said: "It is a pity that so brave a Soldier must vanish."

Meanwhile they were all opening cupboards, wardrobes, and presses, bringing out their daintiest dresses, curling their hair before the mirrors, skipping about, and rejoicing at the prospect of the dance. Only the on a stair before?" Then they went farther and farther down into strange spaces lit only by jewels, till at last they stood in a wonderful avenue of trees, all whose leaves were of silver that shone and glittered like moonlight.

The Soldier thought: "I must carry some token away with me," and broke off a twig from one of those silver branches. As he did so the tree cracked with a loud report, so that he thought for a moment he was back in the wars.

The youngest princess cried out again: "All is not well. Did you hear that sound of warning?"

But the eldest said: "Tush! my heart was never so light. Those are triumphal salutes because we shall soon have set our princes free from enchantment."

Next they came to an avenue where the leaves were all of gold, and then to a third where they were all of dazzling diamonds. The Soldier broke off a twig from a gold branch and another from a diamond branch, and each time there was such a loud crack that the youngest princess cried out in terror, but the eldest laughed at her and still said that these reports were royal salutes.

They went on and on and on until they came to a great lake, like one huge melted sapphire. Here were moored twelve little boats, and in each sat a joyous prince. They were waiting for the twelve princesses, and each took one of them into his boat. Last of all the Soldier, still invisible in his fern-seed cloak, seated himself by the youngest. Soon her prince said: "I can't tell why the boat is so heavy to-night; I must row with all my strength if we are to get across."

"It is all strange to-night," said the youngest princess. "It may be my heart that weighs so heavy in the boat."

On the further side of the lake stood a splendid, brilliantly lighted castle, whence sounded the merry music of elfin horns and bugles. The princes moored their boats, led their ladies into the castle, and there each prince danced with the princess he loved; but the Soldier, all unseen, danced with the eldest princess. When the youngest, whom he liked to tease, had a cup of wine in her hand, he drank it up, so that the cup was empty when she put it to her lips. She was alarmed at the loss of her wine, but the eldest princess danced more madly than ever before.

The ball went on until the cocks began to crow far above their heads on earth. All the white satin shoes were in holes by that time and the dance-music ceased. The princes rowed their ladies back again across the lake, and this time the Soldier seated himself close by the eldest princess. On the shore the royal runaways bade farewell to their princes, promising to return the following night and give them another recess from their enchantment. At sight of the marble stair the Soldier ran on ahead, treading softly as a shadow.

When the twelve princesses were back in their room, he was already snoring so loud that they laughed and said: "No danger for us from this sleepyhead of a soldier." They took off their ball-dresses, laid them away, and set the worn-out shoes beside the beds, then lay down, and were soon lost in happy dreams.

Next morning the Soldier resolved to hold his peace, that he might go with them to their wonderful world again. Everything came to pass just as it had the night before. The twelve princesses danced until their shoes were worn to shreds. The second time he carried an emerald fern away with him as a token and the third time a ruby rose.

So on the fourth morning, when the hour had come for his answer, he took the three twigs, the fern, and the rose, and stood in the throne room before the King, while the twelve princesses crowded behind the door and listened for what he was going to say. When the King put the question: "Where do my twelve daughters dance their shoes to shreds every night?" he answered: "In an underground castle with twelve enchanted princes." Then he related what he had seen and where he had gone, and brought out the tokens.

The King had the heralds call in a loud voice for his daughters, who came out quickly from behind the door. Their father asked them whether the Soldier had told the truth, and like kings' daughters they held up their heads and confessed all. Thereupon the King asked the Soldier which princess he would have as his bride. The youngest shrank away in terror, but he said: "Sire, the most beautiful—the eldest."

So the marriage was celebrated on that very day, and the bewitched princes of the underground castle were set free from their enchantment and danced at the wedding—all except the prince who had been used to dance with the eldest princess. He chose to stay down in the heart of the earth and reign as king in the splendid castle by the sapphire lake.

BEAUTY AND THE BEAST

BEAUTY AND THE BEAST

Once upon a time, there was a merchant who was very, very rich. This merchant had three boys and three girls. The three daughters were all pretty, but the youngest was the prettiest of all. Indeed, she was so beautiful that everyone, during her childhood, called her Little Beauty. When she grew up the name clung to her and this made her sisters jealous.

Now Beauty was not only prettier than her sisters, but she was better tempered, too, and kind and good to all. The elder sisters were proud and haughty and selfish, and would have nothing to do with anyone who was not rich and grand.

One evening the merchant came home tired and sad. He had suddenly lost his huge fortune. He no longer had plenty of money, and their beautiful home, with its lovely lawns, trees and flowers, must be sold. All that was left was a little cottage in the country, and the family must move out there to live. With the tears running down his cheeks the merchant said to his sons and daughters:

"My children, we must go and live in the cottage and we shall have to work hard to earn our living."

The big sisters did not want to go at all, but Beauty was glad, for she loved the country, and liked nothing better than to take long walks through the woods and fields.

When the family was settled in the cottage, the merchant and his three sons worked hard in the fields from sunrise to sunset, and managed to make enough money on which to live. Beauty was a great help to her father. She rose at four o'clock, put the house in order, and got breakfast for the whole family. It was hard at first, for she was not used to working like a servant, but it grew easier and easier, and Beauty grew healthier and rosier. She became a fine little housekeeper, a fine little cook, and a fine little laundress. When she had finished her work, she would amuse herself with reading, or playing on the harpsichord, or spinning the golden flax, singing as she spun.

Her sisters did not know what to do to pass the time. They did not get up until ten o'clock. Then they strolled about, wailing over the loss of their carriage and their fine clothes. And they despised poor Beauty because she was not as miserable as they were.

The family had been living in the cottage about a year when one morning a letter came to the merchant. This letter told him that one of his richest ships, which he had thought lost, had come at last to port.

The two elder sisters were wild with joy. When their father set out for the port they begged he would bring back to them new gowns, caps, rings, and all sorts of trinkets. Beauty asked for nothing, for she thought that all the ship's cargo would scarcely buy what her sisters had asked for.

"Don't you want me to bring you anything, Beauty?" asked her father.

"Since you are so kind as to think of me, dear father," answered Beauty, "I should like to have you bring me a rose, for we have none in our garden."

It was not that Beauty cared so much for a rose, but she did not want it to look as if she were trying to be better than her sisters, who would have said she refused only to be praised.

The father set out on his journey, but when he reached the port he had to go to law about the cargo. After a great deal of trouble he started back as poor as when he left home.

He was within thirty miles of his home, and was thinking of how happy he would be to see his children again. But his road lay through a thick forest, and in a blinding storm he lost his way. All at once, down a long avenue of trees, he saw a golden gleam which seemed to be at a great distance. He rode toward it and found that it shone from a splendid palace brightly lighted from top to bottom. Not a soul was to be seen in any of the outer yards.

The stable door stood open, and the merchant's horse, half-starved, walked in and helped himself to a plentiful meal of oats and hay. Leaving his horse in the stable, the merchant went into the house. Still he found no one. But in a large room he found a cheerful fire and a table spread with the finest food. The table was set for one.

As the rain and snow had wet him to the skin, he went and stood before the fire.

"Surely," he said to himself, "the master of the house or his servants will pardon the liberty I am taking. Of course some one will come before long."

He waited and waited, but no one came. When the clock struck eleven, he decided he could endure his hunger no longer. So he helped himself to a chicken, which he ate to the bones, all the time trembling with fear. Now that he no longer felt hungry, he took courage and began to look about him. He passed through one beautifully furnished room after another, and finally came to a chamber in which there was an inviting couch. It was past midnight and he was very tired, so he shut the door and went to bed.

It was ten o'clock the next morning when he waked. And what was his astonishment to see beside his bed a handsome new suit of clothes, instead of his own, which were quite worn out!

"Surely," he said to himself, "this palace belongs to a good fairy, who

has taken pity on me and cared for me in my trouble."

He looked out of the window and saw no snow, but a lovely flower garden. He returned to the room where he had eaten the night before and there he found a little table spread with fruit and eggs, a plate of buttered toast, and a pot of fragrant hot coffee.

"Thank you, good fairy," he said aloud, "for your kind care of me."

After breakfast he started toward the stable to look after his horse. As he passed through the rose garden he remembered what Beauty had asked for, and he picked a

spray of roses to carry home. As he was picking them he heard a terrible noise, and saw such a frightful beast coming toward him that he almost fainted with fear.

"Ungrateful man!" roared the Beast. "I saved your life by receiving you in my palace, and in return you steal my roses, which I love more than anything else in the world. You shall pay for this with your life."

The merchant threw himself on his knees, crying:

"My lord, forgive me! I did not mean to offend you. I picked only this one spray for my youngest daughter who had asked me to bring her a rose."

"I am not a lord," replied the monster, "but a beast. I do not like sweet words, so do not think you can soften me with flattery. You say you have daughters. I will pardon you if one of them will come and die in your place. Do not try to argue with me, but go; and swear to me that if your daughters refuse, you will come back in three months."

The merchant did not intend for a moment to let one of his daughters die for him. But he thought that if he pretended to do what the

Beast asked he would at least see his children again. So he promised, and the Beast told him he might set off as soon as he pleased.

"But," added the Beast, "I don't want you to go empty-handed. Go back to the room in which you slept. There you will find an empty chest which you may fill with whatever you like best. I will send it to your house."

The Beast then went away, and the merchant said to himself:

"If I must die, I shall at least be able to leave something for my children."

He went back to the room in which he had slept. There he found a great quantity of gold pieces and, after slipping five into his purse, he filled the chest to the very brim with them. Then he mounted his horse and set out for home. The horse found his way through the forest, and in a few hours the merchant reached his cottage. All six children gathered around him. After giving to each of the others a gold piece, he handed to Beauty the spray of roses, saying:

"Take it, Beauty; little do you think what it has cost your poor father."

Then he told them all that had happened in the Beast's palace. The two elder sisters began to weep, and

to blame Beauty, who did not shed a tear.

"See," said they, "what the pride of the little wretch has done! Why did she not ask for fine things as we did? But no, she must do something different! And now she is causing her father's death, yet she does not shed a tear!"

"Why should I weep?" said Beauty. "My father will not die. I shall in his stead give myself up to the Beast."

"No, no, sister!" cried the three brothers. "You shall not die. We will go and find this monster, and he or we will perish."

"You can never kill him," said the merchant. "You have no idea how powerful he is. I cannot thank Beauty enough for her love, but I will not let her die for me."

"You shall never go to the palace without me," cried Beauty. "You cannot prevent my following you."

The merchant was so unhappy at the thought of losing Beauty that he never thought of the chest of gold. But when he went to his room at night, he found it standing by his bedside. He said nothing to his elder daughters about his treasure, for he knew they would want it for dowries to win them husbands, but he told Beauty the secret.

When the three months had passed, the merchant and Beauty set out for the palace of the Beast. The

two sisters rubbed their eyes with an onion to make believe they shed a great many tears, but the merchant and his sons really wept. Beauty did not cry, for she thought this would only make the others more unhappy.

The horse took the right road of his own accord and when they reached the palace, went at once to the stable. Hand in hand, the merchant and Beauty entered the house, and there they found a table set for two, with the most delicious things to eat. After supper they heard a roar like thunder; and the poor merchant wept as he told Beauty good-by, for she had persuaded him, for the sake of his other children, to leave her there alone.

Beauty, when she saw the terrible Beast, all claws and bristles, trembled a little, but she tried to be as brave as she could. The monster asked her if she had come of her own free will.

"Y-e-s," she answered, trembling.

"You are a good girl," growled the Beast, "and I thank you. As for you," he said to the father, who, forgetting his promise had rushed back to protect his child, "you are to leave this place to-morrow morning. Take care that you never find your way here again. Good-night, Beauty!"

"Good-night, Beast!" she answered in her sweet-toned voice, and the monster shuffled away.

"O my child," groaned the merchant, "I cannot leave you to such a fate. Go home and let me stay."

"No," replied Beauty. "What would become of the other children without you? You must go home to-morrow morning."

They now wished each other a sorrowful good-night and went to bed. In the morning the merchant kissed Beauty good-by and rode sadly toward home. When he was out of sight Beauty sat down and cried. But she was really a brave girl and soon dried her tears and began to explore the palace. What was her surprise at coming to a doorway over which was written "Beauty's room!" She opened the door, and her eyes were dazzled by the splendor of the chamber. But she was most pleased with the many books, the harpsichord, and the music.

"Does the Beast want me to be happy?" she wondered. "Surely he would not have done all this for me if I had only one day to live."

She opened a book, in which was written in letters of gold:

"You may wish for anything, you may order anything. You are queen and mistress here."

"Alas!" thought Beauty, "there is nothing I want so much as to see my poor father, and to know what he is doing now."

Just then she glanced at a large looking-glass, and lo and behold! she saw her home, and her father riding up to the cottage. Her sisters had come out to meet him and they were trying to look sorry, but they could not hide their joy because Beauty had not come back. Beauty saw the picture for only a moment, but she began to think that the Beast might mean to be kind to her. Surely she need not be afraid of him!

23

At noon she found dinner served, and as she ate she heard the sweetest music, though she saw no one. That evening Beauty was just sitting down to the supper table when she heard the shuffle of great shaggy paws, and she could not help trembling with terror.

"Beauty," growled the Beast, standing up pleadingly on his hind legs, "will you give me the pleasure of seeing you sup?"

"That is as you wish," answered Beauty.

"Tell me, Beauty," asked the Beast, "do you think I am very, very ugly?"

"Yes, Beast," said Beauty, "I cannot tell a lie. But I think you are very good."

Beauty ate with an excellent appetite, and the Beast was so humble and polite she had nearly got the better of her fear of him when he asked:

"Beauty, will you marry me?"

She was afraid of making the monster angry if she refused, but said bravely:

"No, Beast."

The Beast sighed so deeply that he shook the palace, and sadly said: "Good-night, Beauty!" Then he left her, and Beauty began to feel sorry for him.

"Alas!" she said, "what a pity he is so frightful, since he is so good."

Beauty lived three months in the palace very contentedly. The Beast visited her every evening. Beauty grew used to his ugliness, and every evening she saw more clearly how good he was. But there was one thing that made her unhappy. Every evening before he left her the Beast asked her to marry him. And when, every evening, she said no, his sighs made the palace rock as if in a high wind. At last one night the Beast said to her:

"If you will not marry me, at least promise me, Beauty, that you will never leave me."

"No," said Beauty, weeping, "I will never cause your death. I promise to come back in a week."

"You shall find yourself with your father to-morrow morning," answered the Beast. "But remember your promise. When you wish to come back, just put your ring on a table when you go to bed. Good-by, dear Beauty."

When Beauty awoke in the morning she found herself at home in her father's cottage. Her father was so happy to see Beauty that he almost died of joy. He sent word of her return to the sisters, who came hurrying over with their husbands

Now Beauty, that very day, had seen in her looking-glass that her father had fallen sick of grief, so she said:

"I would willingly promise never to leave you, but I shall die if I cannot go and see my dear father. He is ill and poor. My sisters have found that chest of gold you gave my father, have divided it for dowries and are married, my brothers are away in the army, and he is alone. Oh, please, good Beast, do not refuse me!"

"I would rather die myself, dear Beauty," replied the Beast, "than to make you unhappy. You may go to your father, and your poor Beast shall die of grief."

to pay her a visit. The husband of the eldest sister was extremely handsome; but he was so vain of his good looks that he thought of nothing else from morning till night. The second sister had married a very clever man, but the only use he made of his cleverness was to torment his friends and his wife.

The two sisters were more jealous than ever when they saw Beauty dressed like a princess and looking so very beautiful. They made a plan to end her happiness.

"Let us," said the elder, "try to keep her here after her week's leave is over. The Beast will surely be so angry that he will eat her up in a moment."

So when the week was ended, the two sisters began to tear their hair, and shed so many tears at the thought of Beauty's leaving them that she consented to stay a few days longer. But she could not help feeling sorry for the poor Beast, who was being made so unhappy.

The tenth night that Beauty was in her father's home she dreamed she was strolling in the garden of the palace. On the grass lay the Beast, almost dead. Beauty awoke and burst into tears.

"How wicked I am," she said, "to be so ungrateful to my kind Beast!"

She laid her ring on the table and soon fell asleep again. In the morning she found herself in the Beast's palace. All day she wished for the supper hour, that the Beast might come. She had never passed so long a day. At length the clock struck seven, but no Beast came. Beauty ran from room to room of the palace, calling him, but no one answered. At last she remembered her dream, and ran toward the grass plot on which she had dreamed she saw him. There lay the poor Beast on the grass.

Beauty threw herself on the shaggy body, and finding that his heart was still beating, she ran quickly for water and threw it on his face. The Beast quickly opened his eyes and said:

"You forgot your promise to me, dear Beauty. And my grief was so great that I tried to starve myself to death. Now, Beauty, I shall die happy, for I have seen you once more."

"No, dear Beast," cried Beauty, "you shall not die. You must live to be my husband. I thought I felt only gratitude, but now I know I love you."

As soon as Beauty had said these words, the palace and the garden suddenly blazed with light. Music sounded, fireworks shone. Beauty

turned to look at her dear Beast, but suddenly no Beast was to be seen in the garden. Instead, the very handsomest prince that was ever seen knelt at Beauty's feet and thanked her for having broken his enchantment.

"But where is my dear Beast?" asked Beauty.

"You see him, Beauty, at your feet," answered the Prince. "A wicked fairy had given me the form of a beast, and declared that I must keep it until a beautiful girl should love me and consent to marry me."

Beauty went with the Prince to the palace, where, to her delight, she found her dear father and all her family. Together the happy company traveled to the young Prince's dominions, and there the Prince was received with great joy by his subjects, who had mourned him as lost. The Prince married Beauty, and together they reigned happily for a long, long time.

JACK AND THE GIANT CORMORAN

JACK THE GIANT-KILLER

ONCE upon a time, when Arthur was King of Britain, there lived in a cave of the Mount of Cornwall a huge giant named Cormoran. If three tall men stood on top of one another, they would be just as tall as this giant. He was so fat, too, that it took some time to walk around him.

Now at the foot of this hill where the giant lived there were several farms. When the giant wanted a meal, he took six steps down the mountain and robbed the farmers. Sometimes he carried off half a dozen oxen and a dozen sheep at a time. The oxen he slung over his shoulder, and the sheep he tied around his waist in bunches like radishes.

The poor farmers were almost ruined, but they could think of no way to get rid of the giant. At last a brave boy, called Jack, made up his mind to put an end to these unwelcome visits.

One dark night he dug a huge pit at the foot of the mountain. Across the top of the pit he laid long sticks, and over the sticks he scattered straw, and over the straw he laid a cover of green turf, till no one could know there was a pit beneath. Very early the next morning Jack took his stand on the other side of the pit and blew a loud blast on his cow horn. Tan-ta-ra, tan-ta-ra, tan-ta-ra, sang Jack's horn. Up jumped the giant in a very bad temper.

"Who dares to wake me at this time of day?" he growled. And he rushed out of his cave and down the mountain-side. At the foot of the mountain sat Jack on a big stone. "It was you, was it?" roared the giant, catching sight of Jack. "Well, you shall pay for it, you saucebox," and he dashed toward the boy. But as soon as he stepped on the covering of the pit — crash! He fell to the bottom.

Jack came to the edge of the pit and laughed at wicked old Cormoran, who was slowly picking himself up. When he stood on tip-toe, his head appeared above the broken layer of straw and turf, and he began to try to scramble out. This was Jack's chance. He seized his pickax and struck the giant a terrible blow on that empty skull

of his, so that Cormoran slipped back into the pit dead as a stone.

Soon it was known all round the country-side how clever and how brave Jack had been. The people were all very proud of him, and gave him a sword and belt. On the sword was the name "Jack the Giant-Killer," and on the belt was written in gold letters:

"This is the valiant Cornishman
Who slew the giant Cormoran."

Another giant, named Blunderbore, vowed that he would punish Jack for killing Cormoran, but Jack knew nothing about this. Before long, while on his way to Wales,

Jack reached a dark, lonely forest. Through the trees he spied a castle and thought he would visit it, but as he was tired, he sat down to rest before going on to the castle. And as he rested, he fell asleep.

Now the castle Jack saw was an enchanted castle, and belonged to the giant Blunderbore. Jack had not been asleep very long when Blunderbore came by. As he had just had dinner he might have passed the sleeping boy, but he saw the two lines of writing on his belt:

"This is the valiant Cornishman
Who slew the giant Cormoran."

"Ha-ha!" he said, "I've been looking for you!" And he picked Jack up and put him in his pocket as if Jack boy were only a jack-knife.

When Jack woke and found himself all doubled up in a giant's pocket, he was so frightened that he shook from head to toe. The giant felt him tremble and knew he was awake.

"Ha-ha, he-he, ho-ho! So you killed my brother Cormoran, did you? Now I'll kill you. Ha-ha, he-he, ho-ho!" And the giant laughed so loud that Jack felt as if he were in the middle of an earthquake.

When they reached the castle, Blunderbore picked Jack out of his pocket between thumb and finger, locked him in a room upstairs, and went off to bring another giant to supper. Jack rubbed himself for a minute and then looked round and round the room. Surely there must be some way out! But he could find none. At last he saw in one corner a coil of rope, and an idea struck him. He uncoiled the rope and made two big nooses, with slip-knots. Then he stood by the window and watched.

Sure enough, here came the giants. They were walking slowly, arm in arm, and the path along which they went passed close under Jack's window. As they drew near, Jack heard Blunderbore say: "This morning I found a plump lad in the forest, that same young scamp who killed our brother Cormoran. We'll have him for supper, broiled in butter."

"You will, will you?" thought Jack. Just at that moment the two giants were right under his window. Quick as lightning Jack flung down his rope with its slipknots. One noose dropped over the head of Blunderbore and one over the head of his guest. Jack pulled with might and main, and in two minutes the giants were strangled.

Then Jack slid down from the window on the rope. He took from

Blunderbore's pocket a big bundle of keys — the keys that had given him so many bumps and bruises when he was traveling with them — and went prowling about. One key unlocked the door of a room where three beautiful ladies were tied up by their hair. Jack untied them, made a low bow, and said: "Ladies, the castle with all it contains is now yours." Doing up their hair as fast as they could, they bowed in return and thanked him. Then he went on his way to Wales.

After Jack had gone through the forest and climbed over a mountain, he found himself in a lonely valley.

could cut through anything. The shoes could rush as quickly as the wind. Jack made up his mind to get all four of them.

'It is worth while risking a good deal to win these wonderful things," said Jack to himself, as he followed the giant into the castle. The giant politely led him to a big room with a fine soft bed. But Jack couldn't sleep. Before long he heard the giant's voice in the next room grumbling:

"Though here with me you lodge
   to-night,
You shall not see the morning light;
My club shall dash your brains out
   quite."

"We'll see about that," said Jack, slipping out of bed. In the corner he found a log of wood just his size. He put it into the bed, tucked it up, and hid himself in a corner.

Soon the door softly opened and the two-headed giant stole in. "I'll make short work of you," he muttered, and he brought down his club time after time on what he supposed was Jack's body. Finally he went away whistling, sure that he had killed Jack.

The next morning Jack, cool as a cucumber, walked into the room where the giant sat at breakfast. Of course the giant could hardly believe his eyes when he saw the boy, but he pretended not to be surprised.

He was hoping he might come to a cottage where he could rest for the night, but suddenly, turning a corner, he found himself in front of a splendid castle. As he was too tired to go farther, Jack knocked at the door. It was opened at once by a huge Welsh giant with two heads.

Now as soon as Jack set eyes on him, he remembered he had heard that this giant owned four valuable things. These were a wonderful coat, a wonderful cap, a wonderful sword, and a wonderful pair of shoes. The coat made the wearer invisible. The cap told him whatever he wanted to know. The sword

"I hope you slept well," he said, watching Jack closely with those four crafty eyes.

"Pretty well, thank you," answered Jack. "I was disturbed a little. A rat ran across my bed and slapped me three or four times with its tail, but I soon dropped off to sleep again."

The giant was very much puzzled. How could he have given those terrible blows with his club and not smashed every bone in Jack's body? That was a question he could not answer, but you may be sure he did not ask Jack. He did invite him to breakfast, though, and placed before him a great bowl of hasty pudding. Jack wanted the giant to

think he could eat as much as anybody, so he managed to fasten a leather bag under his loose coat. Then, when the giant thought Jack was eating, most of the pudding went past the boy's mouth into the hidden bag.

After breakfast Jack said to the giant: "Can you do as clever tricks as I can? I can cut myself open and let out my breakfast without hurting myself." Then he ripped up the leather bag with a knife, and the pudding fell out on the floor.

The giant did not like to be beaten by a little fellow like Jack, so he said: "Of course I can cut myself open, if you can."

With these words he plunged his knife into his body and fell down dead. And Jack, of course, helped himself to the wonderful coat and cap and sword and shoes; for it was a law in King Arthur's days that anybody who killed a giant might have all the giant's things.

Once more Jack started on his travels, and once more he reached a lonely castle and asked for a night's lodging. This time he was welcomed by many knights and ladies, who invited him to have supper with them. It was a merry company, and Jack was enjoying himself very much when a messenger rushed in to say the two-headed giant Thunderdale was on his way up to the castle. Jack put on his cap, which whispered to him what to do, and at once he sprang up and ran out.

Now this castle was surrounded by a deep moat, and to reach the castle or to leave it one had to cross the moat by a drawbridge. Jack quickly set men at work sawing this drawbridge nearly through, so that it could not bear a heavy weight. Next he put on his coat that made him invisible, and his shoes that could carry him as fast as the wind. He then crossed the bridge to meet the giant, carrying in his hand the sword that could cut through anything.

The giant could not see Jack because of the wonderful coat, but he sniffed the air and chanted in a voice like thunder:

"Fe, fi, fo, fum,
 I smell the blood of an Englishman;
 Be he alive, or be he dead,
 I'll grind his bones to make my bread."

"Oh, ho, you will, will you, Mr. Miller?" cried Jack. "Well, you must catch me first." Then he threw off his coat and ran before the giant; and every now and again he all but let himself be caught, just to tease. But he took care to make good use of his shoes of swiftness, and to keep out of reach. The giant was almost beside himself with rage as he chased Jack round and round the castle.

The lords and ladies watched from one of the towers, and clapped their hands as they saw Jack lead the giant such a dance. At last Jack sprang across the drawbridge. The giant followed, but beneath his monstrous body the cut bridge snapped and the giant was hurled headlong into the moat beneath. Jack stood on the edge of the moat and poked fun at him.

"I thought you were going to grind my bones to make your bread," said Jack. "Why don't you begin?"

The giant foamed with rage but could say nothing, for both his mouths were full of the ditch water and mud.

Then Jack threw a strong rope over the heads of the giant, and with a team of oxen dragged him to the edge of the moat. Next he drew his magic sword and cut off the giant's two heads with one mighty stroke.

And you may be sure that ringing cheers of "Long live Jack the Giant-Killer!" echoed through the castle.

After spending some time with the lords and ladies, Jack set out on his last adventure. He went over hill and dale without meeting any one till he came to a little hut at the foot of a high mountain. He knocked, and the door was opened by an old man with hair as white as snow.

"I have lost my way, good father," said Jack. "Can you give me a night's lodging?"

"Gladly, good son," said the old man, "if you can be content with humble fare."

Jack said he would be grateful for a meal of any kind, and gladly ate the bread and fruit set before him.

After supper the old man said solemnly, "My son, your belt tells me you are Jack the Giant-Killer. A task lies before you. At the top of this mountain is an enchanted castle which belongs to a giant called Galligantus. Whenever knights or fair ladies approach his castle he calls a wicked magician, by whose

help he changes them into beasts. But worse still, not very long ago Galligantus and the magician strolled into the garden of the Duke who lives in a neighboring valley. There they saw the beautiful daughter of the Duke gathering flowers. The magician spoke a magic word, and instantly a chariot drawn by two fairy dragons appeared in the garden. The giant snatched up the lady, set her down in the chariot, and, before she had time even to cry out, the dragons flew away with her through the air to the enchanted castle. There she was changed into a white deer, and a deer she must remain until the enchantment is broken. This is the task that lies before you, my son."

"Gladly will I undertake it," cried Jack.

Next morning he put on his magic cap and coat and shoes, and took his magic sword in his hand. His cap told him the way and in a moment his shoes, swift as wings, had brought him to the castle gate. Because he had on his coat of darkness, the two fiery dragons that guarded the gate did not see him, and he passed safely between them.

On the door hung a golden trumpet. Under it were written these words:

"Whoever can this trumpet blow
Shall soon the giant overthrow."

When Jack read this, he seized the trumpet and blew a tremendous blast. The frightened door at once flew open and Jack entered the castle. The giant and the magician, sitting together at the breakfast table, stared at him open-mouthed, unable to move, for they knew that the blast of the golden horn meant the end of their wicked work.

Jack lost no time in drawing his magic sword, and in a moment the giant Galligantus tumbled from his chair and lay dead upon the floor. Just as he fell, a whirlwind rushed through the castle, carrying away the magician. Instantly the enchanted birds and beasts in the garden all became the knights and ladies they had been before. The white deer that had been tied to a haw-thorn tree vanished, and there was the Duke's daughter, as beautiful as ever, crowned with a wreath of pink hawthorn blossoms.

Jack led the knights and ladies down the mountain-side, and when they looked around for a last view of the castle, lo and behold, there was nothing but mist!

At the foot of the mountain the old hermit welcomed them joyfully, and they rested with him for a while. Then they all traveled together to King Arthur's court. You may be sure the King was glad to hear Jack tell of his wonderful adventures with Cormoran, with Blunderbore, with the Welsh giant, with Thunderdale, and, best of all, with the giant Galligantus.

Then Jack's fame spread through the whole country, and one day the Duke said to him: "I should like to have you marry my daughter." As this was what Jack wanted more than anything else in the world, he said he was willing to oblige the Duke. So for the rest of his life he lived in happiness and, to save his wife from worrying, sought out no more adventures, although he was always known, far and wide in the land, as "JACK THE GIANT-KILLER."

DON'T BE AFRAID, BOYS

HOP O' MY THUMB

Once upon a time there was a poor woodcutter who had seven children, all boys. The eldest was ten, the youngest only seven. This youngest was a tiny chap—indeed, he was the smallest person ever seen. When he was born he was no bigger than his father's thumb, so everybody called him Hop o' my Thumb. Little Hop o' my Thumb almost never said a word, so nobody guessed how very much cleverer he was than any of his six brothers. For though he spoke only once in a while and said but little, he heard everything that went on.

The woodcutter and his wife at last became so poor they could no longer give their children enough to eat. One evening, when the boys were in bed, the husband said with a deep sigh:

"You see, my dear wife, we can find food for our children no longer. I cannot bear to see them die of hunger before my eyes, so I am going to take them into the forest tomorrow morning and leave them there. We will slip away from them, and they can never find their way back home."

"Oh!" cried the poor wife, "you surely cannot mean to leave your own children to perish!"

But her husband kept telling her to think how dreadful it would be to see the boys die of hunger before her very eyes, and at last the poor woman gave consent, and went weeping to bed.

Now Hop o' my Thumb had been awake all the time. When he heard his father talking so earnestly he slipped away from his brothers and hid behind his father's chair, to hear without being seen. When his father and mother stopped talking, he stole quietly back to bed and lay awake all night, trying to decide what he should do. In the morning he rose early and ran down to the stream. There he filled his pockets with smooth white pebbles and then hurried back home.

Soon they all set out for the forest, and Hop o' my Thumb said never a word about what he had heard. They went deep into the woods, and the woodcutter set to work chopping down trees, while the children gathered twigs for fagots. When the father and mother saw the boys were

all busy, they slipped away quietly and went home by a bypath.

Soon the children found that they were alone, and began to cry at the top of their voices. Hop o' my Thumb let them cry for a while, but he smiled to himself. He knew how to lead them safely home! For had he not, as they came into the woods, dropped the white pebbles he had in his pocket all along the path? At last he said:

"Don't be afraid, boys. Father and mother have left us here by ourselves, but I can lead you back home again."

The brothers kept close to Hop o' my Thumb, who followed the pebbles, step by step, and so brought them to their father's house. They were afraid to go in, but they peeped through the window. Now it happened that just as the woodman and his wife reached home without their children, a great lord, galloping by, tossed them a piece of gold. The woodcutter sent his wife out to buy meat; and because she was so used to a large family, she bought enough for nine instead of two. When they had eaten all they wanted, she cried:

"Alas! where are our children? How they would feast on what we have left! Where are our children, our poor children?"

She said this so loud that the children, listening at the door, heard her, and cried out together, "Here we are, mother, here we are!"

The mother ran to let them in and kissed them all fondly: "How glad I am to see you, you little rogues!" she cried. "Are you not tired and hungry? Come in to dinner!"

The seven children sat down at the table and ate everything that was left. The parents looked on with delight,—a delight that lasted until the gold was all spent. Then they made up their minds they would have to lose their seven sons once more.

"This time," said the father, "we will take them much deeper into the forest, so they cannot find their way out."

They talked in whispers, but again Hop o' my Thumb heard all they said. Of course he thought he could do just what he did before; but when he slipped out of bed to get his white pebbles, he found that the door was double locked. Hop o' my Thumb did not know what to do. But when his mother gave him a piece of bread for breakfast, he made up his mind that this should take the place of the pebbles, and he put it into his pocket.

The father and mother took care, this time, to lead the children into the very thickest and darkest part of the forest. They left them there, and went home by a bypath as before. Hop o' my Thumb did not worry; he was sure he could find his way back by means of the crumbs he had scattered along the path. But to his surprise, not a morsel was left! The birds had come and eaten those crumbs all up!

The poor children were now in a terrible plight. The harder they tried to find their way out, the deeper they went into the forest. Night came on, and the wind began to howl. They thought it was the howling of wolves, and every moment they expected a wild beast to jump out and seize them.

Hop o' my Thumb climbed to the top of a tree and looked all about.

Far, far off, beyond the forest, he saw a little light, like a candle. When he came down he could not see it, but the children all started to walk in the direction in which he had seen the light. At last they reached the end of the forest, and the light shone out again. They hurried toward it, and finally reached a house from which the little light came. They knocked softly at the door and a big, pleasant-faced woman opened it, and asked them what they wanted.

"We are poor children," said Hop o' my Thumb. "We have lost our way in the woods. Please, please, let us come in and lie down until morning."

The woman, looking at their pleading childish faces, began to cry, and sobbed: "Oh, you poor children! What a place for you to come to! This is the house of an Ogre who eats little boys and girls."

"Deary me!" exclaimed Hop o' my Thumb, "what shall we do? If we go back to the woods, the wolves will surely eat us. We would rather stay here and be eaten by the Ogre. Maybe when he sees us he will be kind to us, if you coax him hard."

The Ogre's wife built no hope on her coaxing, but thought perhaps she could hide the boys from her husband till morning; so she let them in. She told them to warm themselves by the fire, before which there was a whole sheep roasting for the ogre's supper. While they were standing by the fire there came a loud knocking at the door. It was the Ogre! His wife hid the children under the bed and told them to lie still. Then she let her husband in.

"Is supper ready?" demanded the Ogre.

"Yes, all ready," replied his wife; and she put the sheep on the table before him. Pretty soon he began to sniff, and said: "I smell fresh meat."

"It must be the calf which has just been killed," answered his wife.

"I smell the flesh of a child," roared the Ogre. "There is something here that is hidden from the master of the house."

With these words, he jumped up from the table and went straight to the bed.

"Aha, wicked woman, so these are your tricks, are they?" he jeered,

reaching under the bed and feeling the children. "If you weren't so tough, old wife, I would eat you, too! But after all, this is lucky enough, for the brats will make a nice dish for the three Ogres, my special friends, who are to dine with me tomorrow."

His big, rough hands drew out the children one by one from under the bed. They fell on their knees, begging him to spare them. But this Ogre was the cruelest of all the Ogres, and he was already devouring them with his eyes. "Yes," he said to his wife, "they will be delicious morsels if you serve them up with a savory sauce."

Then he fetched a large knife and began to sharpen it on a whetstone, while the children shook with fear. Roughly snatching up one of the seven, he was just about to cut the boy to pieces, when his wife said to him:

"Why take the trouble to kill them tonight? Won't tomorrow be time enough?"

"Hold your tongue!" thundered the Ogre. "They will be tenderer for the keeping."

"But you have so much meat in the house already," answered his wife — "a calf, two sheep, and half a pig."

"That's so," said the Ogre. "Give them a good supper to fatten them up a bit, and send them to bed."

So the kind woman set a good supper before them, but the poor children were too badly frightened to eat. As for the Ogre, he sat

down to his wine, chuckling over the thought of the treat in store for himself and his monster friends. And before long he stumbled off to bed.

Now this Ogre had seven daughters, all very young. They had fair complexions, because they ate raw meat, like their father; but they had small, round, gray eyes, hooked noses, wide mouths, and very long, sharp teeth set far apart. They were too young to have done a great deal of mischief, but they gave signs of being as cruel as the old Ogre himself, for they already delighted in biting little children. These young ogresses had gone to sleep early, all in one large bed. Each one had a little gold crown on her head. In their room was another bed, just the same size, and in this the Ogre's wife put the seven little boys, tying nightcaps under their chins. Of course, Hop o' my Thumb's bright eyes noticed that the young Ogresses all had gold crowns on their heads.

As he lay wide awake beside his sleeping brothers, Hop o' my Thumb began to be afraid the Ogre would feel sorry he had not killed them all that night. So about midnight he slid out of bed, took off the seven nightcaps, and crept over to the bed where the Ogre's daughters were sound asleep. He lifted off their gold crowns and tied the nightcaps on their heads instead; and then he put the crowns on himself and his brothers, and climbed back into bed.

"He will feel the crowns," thought Hop o' my Thumb, "and think we are his daughters."

Everything went just as he hoped. Soon after midnight the Ogre waked, sorry he had put off till the next day making ready for his feast. So he sprang out of bed and again whetted his knife till it was sharp enough to cut open his own hard heart.

"Now we'll see," he growled, "what these young rogues are about, and do the job at once!"

He stalked up to the room in which his daughters slept, and stole to the bed that held the boys. They were all fast asleep except Hop o' my Thumb. The Ogre passed his hand over the boys' heads one by one and felt the gold crowns.

"That would have been a pretty mistake!" he said. He went next to his daughters' bed and, feeling the nightcaps, grunted: "Here you are, you young rascals!" Then he killed all his daughters, one by one, without waking them at all, and went back to bed well satisfied with himself.

As soon as Hop o my Thumb heard the Ogre snoring, he woke his brothers and told them to put on their clothes and follow him. They

stole down to the garden and jumped from the wall into the road. They ran with all their might, almost all night without in the least knowing where they were going.

When the Ogre woke in the morning, he said to his wife: "Up, woman! Go and dress those tender lads I saw last night."

The Ogress was surprised at her husband's kindness, for she did not dream what he meant by *dressing* the boys. She went upstairs, and almost fainted when she saw her seven daughters all lying dead. The Ogre followed his wife to hurry her about the dinner, and was as amazed as she at what he saw.

"Oh, what have I done?" cried he. "They shall pay for this, the tricky runaways, before many minutes have passed!" Then the Ogre turned to his wife and cried: "Bring me my seven-league boots. I'll catch the little scamps!"

The Ogre set out with all speed, and strode about over the country looking for the boys. At last he turned into the road along which the poor children were hurrying toward their father's house. When they had almost reached it they saw the Ogre stalking from mountain top to

mountain top, and crossing rivers at one step. Hop o' my Thumb made his brothers crawl into a hollow in a rock, and then crept in himself. But you may be sure he kept his eye on the Ogre, to see what he would do next.

Now seven-league boots are very tiring, and the Ogre dropped down to rest on the very rock in which the children lay hidden. He fell asleep, and soon began to snore so loudly that the little fellows were as frightened as when the Ogre bent over them with the knife in his hand. But brave Hop o' my Thumb whispered to his brothers: "Run on home while he is asleep. I must stay here and see what he does."

The brothers did not need to be told twice, and were very soon at their father's house. In the meantime, Hop o' my Thumb went softly up to the Ogre, gently pulled off the seven-league boots, and drew them on his own legs. The boots seemed very large on the Ogre, but they were fairies, and could make themselves small enough to fit anyone. No sooner had Hop o' my Thumb put on the boots than he heard a friendly voice saying:

"Listen, Hop o' my Thumb! The boots you took from the Ogre are two fairies, my brother and I. We are pleased with your courage and your cleverness, and are ready to help you. Go to the Ogre's house, and when the Ogress opens the door, say:

'Ogress, Ogre cannot come;
Great key give to Hop o' my
Thumb.'"

Hop o' my Thumb repeated the two lines over and over that he might not forget them. When he was sure he had learned them by heart, he took two or three of his longest strides and reached the Ogre's door. He knocked loudly and the door was quickly opened by the Ogre's wife. When she saw Hop o' my Thumb she started back and would have shut the door; but Hop o' my Thumb cried out at once:

"Ogress, Ogre cannot come;
Great key give to Hop o' my
Thumb."

The Ogress, seeing her husband's boots, thought the Ogre must have sent Hop o' my Thumb on this errand. So she brought the great key and gave it to him, and even told him where to find the chest of money and jewels to which the key belonged. Hop o' my Thumb took a handful or two, enough to keep his father and mother and brothers in plenty for the rest of their lives, but left the chest still almost full for the Ogress, in return for her kindness to him and his brothers.

Of course, Hop o' my Thumb's family was very glad to see him.

The fame of his boots spread to the court, and the King sent for him, it is said, and employed him in many important affairs of the kingdom.

As for the wicked Ogre, he fell in his sleep from the corner of the rock from which Hop o' my Thumb and the other boys had escaped, and broke his wicked neck. When Hop o' my Thumb heard of his death, he told the King of all that the good-natured Ogress had done to save the lives of the seven lost children. The King was so pleased that he invited the Ogress to his court and bestowed on her the honorable title of Duchess of Draggletail.

FURBALL MADE READY TO SLIP OUT INTO THE WORLD

FURBALL

Once upon a time there was a Princess whose hair was of pure gold. She was the most beautiful maiden on earth and as good as she was beautiful. But she was often sad because her mother had died. Her father, the King, promised her hand to an Ogre, who in return agreed to give the King fifty wagons of silver.

When the Princess heard of her father's bargain she was greatly alarmed, and begged him not to make her so unhappy. But nothing could change his mind. His daughter, however, had quick wits and she said to her father: "Before I marry I must have three bridal gifts—a dress as golden as the sun, another as silvery as the moon, and a third as glittering as the stars. I shall want, besides, a coat made of a thousand different kinds of fur. Every animal in the kingdom must give a part of his skin to make that coat."

"There!" she thought, "I have asked for things which he cannot get, and so he will have to give up his wicked plan."

But the King at once began to provide for the bridal gifts. The most skillful weavers in all the land were sent for and ordered to weave the three dresses, one to be as golden as the sun, another as silvery as the moon, and a third as glittering as the stars. Hunters were sent into the forest to kill wild animals and bring home their skins, of which the coat was to be made. At last, when they were all ready, the King laid them before his daughter and said: "To-morrow your marriage shall take place."

Then the poor Princess saw there was no hope of changing her father's heart, and that her only way of escape from the Ogre was to run away.

In the night, when all the castle was still, she rose from her bed. The sun, moon, and star dresses she folded into a packet so small that she could shut them up in a walnut shell. Then she put on the fur coat, stained her face and hands dark brown with walnut juice, and slipped out into the world.

After traveling all night, she came just at dawn to a large forest. She was very tired, so she crept into a hollow tree and went to sleep. The sun rose higher and higher but still she slept on, and did not awake until nearly noon.

Now on this very day the young King to whom the wood belonged was hunting in the forest. His hounds came to the tree where the Princess slept, and began to sniff about and run round and round the tree, barking eagerly. The King called to his hunters and said: "Look sharp, and see what sort of game hides in that hollow tree."

Two hunters ran to see. When they came back, they told the King that in the hollow tree there was the most wonderful creature ever seen. "It is sound asleep," they

said, "and its body is covered with a thousand different kinds of fur."

"Go and see," said the King, "whether you cannot capture it alive. Bind it on the wagon and bring it to the castle."

While the hunters were binding the maiden, she awoke and cried out in terror. "Who and what are you?" they asked.

"I am only a motherless child, driven from my home," she replied. "Have mercy on me, and take me with you!"

"Well," they said, "you may be useful to the cook, little Furball. We will take you with us; you can at least sweep up the ashes."

So they placed her on the wagon and took her to the King's castle. There they showed her a kennel under the steps, where no daylight ever came, and said: "Furball, here you may live and sleep." Then the Princess was sent into the kitchen to fetch the wood, draw the water, stir the fire, pluck the fowls, clean the vegetables, sweep the ashes, and do all the hard, dirty work.

Poor Furball lived for a long time as a servant of servants. She could not see how this life was ever to end, and how she was ever to be a king's daughter again. One day she heard that a festival was to take place in the castle, so she said

to the cook: "May I go out for a little while to see the guests arrive? I promise you no one shall catch sight of little Furball."

"Go," the gruff old cook replied, "but in half an hour I shall want you to sweep up the ashes and put the kitchen in order."

Then Furball took her smoky oil lamp, ran into her kennel, threw off the fur coat, and washed the nut stains from her face and hands. Oh, but she was beautiful to see! She opened the nutshell, took out the dress that was golden as the sun, and put it on. It lighted up the kennel so that the lamp was ashamed and its smoky flame went out.

As soon as the Princess was dressed, she slipped around to the front of the castle and entered the great door as a guest. No one recognized her as Furball; the door-keepers thought she was a princess from some far country and they quickly told the King of her arrival. He hastened to meet her, bowed low to kiss her hand, and led her out to dance. While they danced he thought in his heart: "Never before have mine eyes seen any maiden so beautiful as this." And as they danced he slipped a gold ring on her finger.

As soon as the dance was over the **Sun Princess** curtesied to the King,

smiled on him so brightly that his eyes were dazzled, and then vanished. The sentinel at the castle gate was called and questioned, but he had seen no one pass.

The Princess had run like a sunbeam to her kennel, taken off the gleaming dress, stained her face and hands, put on her fur coat, and was again Furball. When she entered the kitchen and reached for the broom to sweep up the ashes, the cook said: "Let that go until tomorrow; I want you to make some soup for the King. I am too busy. But do not let one of your hairs drop into the soup, or you will get nothing to eat for a week."

Furball made the King's soup as nicely as she could and toasted bread for it. When the soup was ready, she dropped the King's gold ring into the bowl.

After the ball was over, the King called for his supper, and declared he had never tasted better soup in his life. But when the dish was nearly empty, he saw, to his surprise, the gold ring at the bottom. He could not imagine how it came there, so he ordered the cook to appear before him.

The old cook was in a terrible fright when he heard the order. "You must have let a hair fall into the soup," he growled to Furball. "If you have, I shall give you a good beating and nothing to eat for a week."

As soon as the cook came shuffling into the banquet hall, the King demanded: "Who made this soup?"

"I made it, sire," faltered the frightened cook.

"That is not true," said the King. "This soup is much better than any soup of yours."

Then the cook had to confess that Furball made the soup.

"Go and send her to me," commanded the King.

As soon as ever little Furball appeared, all smutty from the kitchen, the King said to her: "Who are you, maiden, and of what mother born?"

"I am a poor, motherless child, a stranger in your kingdom, Sire," she replied.

"How came you in my castle?" he asked again.

"I serve the royal cook for shelter and for food."

"How came this ring in the soup?"

But Furball only looked at him and would not say a word.

When the King found he could learn nothing from her, he sent her away.

A few weeks later there was another festival, and Furball again begged leave from the cook to go and see the guests arrive at the great door of the palace.

"Go," he grunted, "but be sure you come back in a half hour and make for the King that soup he is so fond of."

She promised to obey, and ran quickly into her little kennel. There she washed off the walnut stains, took out of the nutshell her dress silvery as the moon, and put it on.

Again she appeared at the castle door like a foreign princess, and again the King came to meet her. He was so glad to see her that he would dance with no one else, and while they were dancing he pinned a tiny gold spinning wheel in her hair. But at the end of a half hour she disappeared so suddenly that the King could not imagine what had become of her. Like a moonbeam she slipped around the castle to her kennel, made herself again

the dark-faced, rough-coated little Furball, and went into the kitchen to make the King's soup.

When the soup was ready, she dropped the tiny gold spinning wheel into the bowl. The King ate the soup with great relish, but was amazed to find the gold spinning wheel in the bottom of the bowl. Again he sent for the cook and asked who made the soup, and again the cook had to confess that it was Furball. She was ordered to appear before the King, but when he asked her about the gold spinning wheel, Furball only looked at him and would not say a word.

At the King's third festival everything happened as before. The cook, when he told her she might go and see the guests arrive, growled: "Be back in time for the King's soup. I believe you are a witch. Your soup is good. The King says it is better than I can make; it can only be witchcraft that outdoes my cookery."

Furball did not stop to listen. She ran quickly to her little kennel, washed off the nut stains, and this time clad herself in the dress that glittered like the stars. When the King stepped forward quickly to receive her in the hall, as he had done twice before, he thought her the most beautiful maiden he had ever seen in all his life. While he held her hand in the dance, the King contrived to catch a gold hook into her sleeve.

He had given orders that the dancing should continue longer than usual, but the minute the music stopped Furball slipped her hand from the King's and was gone like a shooting star.

She was out of breath when she reached her kennel under the steps. She had stayed away longer than a half hour, she knew, and there was not time to take off her star dress. She threw her fur coat over it, and began to stain her face and hands. But she was in such a hurry that one finger remained white. When she reached the kitchen she made the King's soup and dropped into it the gold hook.

The King, when he found the small gold hook at the bottom of his bowl, sent at once for Furball, and as she entered the room he saw one white finger shining out from her little brown hand. He seized the hand and held her fast, while she struggled so to get free that the fur coat fell open and the glittering star dress came to view. The King drew off that coat of a thousand furs, and as he did so a flood of wonderful golden hair fell over the maiden's shoulders. She wiped the soot and stains from her face and hands, and stood before the King as the most glorious Princess on earth.

"You shall be my bride," said the young King, "for yours is the beauty of the sun and the moon and the stars."

Then the Princess told him all her story, and he loved her more than before. The next day the wedding took place, the cook made the best bridal soup he could, and the King and his beautiful Queen lived happy ever after.

THE CROSS FAIRY'S GIFT TO THE PRINCESS

BRIAR ROSE OR THE SLEEPING BEAUTY

Once upon a time there lived a King and Queen who grieved because they had no child. Finally a daughter was born to them, and the King was so happy that he gave a great christening feast. As godmothers for his little daughter he asked all the fairies but one in the kingdom. Seven he asked, but the bad-tempered fairy he left out. He hoped that each, after the fairy custom, would give the Princess a gift.

From the christening the company returned to the palace, where a splendid feast had been prepared. Before each fairy was placed a crinkled emerald plate, like a clover leaf, set with diamonds like dewdrops. Just as they were taking their places at the table, in came the cross fairy who had not been invited. She rode into the hall on a snapdragon, for the slight had made her crosser than ever. The King had a plate of pure pearl like a lily petal set before her, but she angrily pushed it away and looked enviously at the emerald plates, which had been made to order for the seven fairies. The cross fairy thought herself ill-treated, and muttered threats under her breath. One of the wisest fairies, who was seated near her, heard these threats, and felt sure she meant to do some harm to the little Princess.

When the company rose from the table, this wise fairy hid behind the cradle, that she might speak last and perhaps undo some of the harm which she knew was brewing in the bad-tempered fairy's mind.

Now the fairies began to give their gifts to the Princess. The youngest gave her beauty; the next, wit; the third, grace; the fourth, virtue; the fifth, a lovely voice; the sixth, a smile to win all hearts.

Then it was the cross fairy's turn. With her ivory wand pointed like a spear at the royal baby, she cried out:

"The King's daughter in her rosebud youth shall prick her hand with a spindle, and fall down dead!"

Everybody fell a-crying with fright at this terrible gift, and as for the poor Queen, she instantly fainted away. But just then the wise fairy popped up from behind the cradle and said: "Be comforted, O King! Revive, O Queen! My gift is still to

with her maids. While the maids were enjoying a gossip with the gardeners, the Princess went roaming about the palace, exploring one room after another. At last she came to an old tower, and at the top of the tower she found a little room in which an old woman sat busily spinning. This old woman had never heard of the King's proclamation.

"Good day, granny!" said the Princess. "What are you doing?"

"I am spinning, my pretty lass," said the old woman, who did not recognize her.

"That is charming!" the Princess cried. "How do you do it? Let me see whether I can spin!"

She caught at the whirling spindle. But because she was too eager, or because a fairy's decree *must* be fulfilled, the spindle pricked her hand and she dropped to the floor in a faint.

The old woman, greatly alarmed, cried for help. People came running from all sides. The gardeners threw water in the face of the Princess. The maids loosened her clothes, and beat her hands, and bathed her temples, but nothing could rouse her.

Then the King and Queen, who had heard the alarm, came too. They knew at once the fairy's evil wish had been fulfilled. They had the Princess carried to a most beautiful

come. I cannot undo entirely what this unkind fairy has done. Your daughter will prick her hand with the spindle and fall to the floor, but instead of dying she will sink into a deep sleep which will last a hundred years. From that sleep, when her dream is over, a king's son shall waken her."

Yet the King hoped to save his dear child from the threatened evil; so he had his heralds proclaim that no one in all the country should spin, or even have a spindle in the house, on pain of death.

When the Princess was fifteen or sixteen years old, the King and Queen went one day to one of their country houses, leaving the Princess room, deep in the heart of the palace, and laid on a bed decked with rose and silver coverlets.

She might have been an angel as she lay there, for her deep sleep had not driven away her lovely color. Her cheeks and lips were as pink as briar roses, her forehead fair as a lily. Her eyes were closed but she breathed softly, and it was easy to see that happy dreams played beneath her eyelids. The King commanded that she be left to sleep in peace until the hour of her awakening had come.

Now the wise fairy whose quick wit had saved the life of the Princess, was thousands of miles away,

but she knew what had happened and came at once in her chariot of golden fire, drawn by eagles. She was afraid the Princess would be frightened and lonesome if she should awaken all alone in an empty, crumbling castle. So this is what she did.

She touched with her wand everything and everybody about the palace, except the King and Queen. She touched the governesses and the ladies in waiting, the gentlemen, the officers, the stewards, cooks, guards, and pages; she touched those weeping maids and shame-faced gardeners; she touched the horses in the stables, the great mastiff in the yard, and the Princess's tiny poodle which lay on the bed beside her. And as she touched them they all fell asleep, not to waken until their mistress should wake, so that they might all

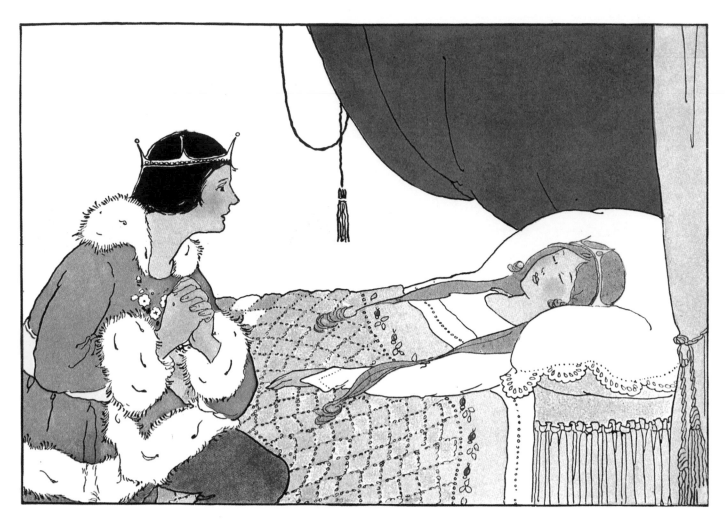

attend upon her. Even the fire slept, and the spit that stood before it full of half-roasted partridges and pheasants. It all took but a moment, for the fairies work quickly.

Then the King and Queen, having kissed their daughter, left the hushed palace. The King issued a new proclamation, forbidding anyone to approach its gates, but such laws were not needed, for in half an hour there had sprung up about the palace a hedge of thorny shrubs, and year by year these grew into trees so thick and high that neither beast nor man could force a way through.

The castle itself was hidden. Only the top of the tower could be seen from a distance.

On the very day that the hundred years ended, the son of the king then reigning was a-hunting, and spied the tower beyond the thorny wood. He asked what it was, and many strange stories were related, but finally an old peasant told him the true tale of the sleeping princess and of the king's son who was to waken her. The Prince felt very sure, from the way his heart began beating, that *he* was the king's son who was to have that wonderful adventure, and he set out at once for the wood. And when he reached it the great trees and the thorns opened of their own accord to let him pass, but closed behind him, so that even his companions could not pass through.

He came at last to the courtyard of the palace, over which hung an utter silence. Nothing living was to be seen but men and animals in profound slumber. The Prince crossed the court and mounted the stairs. In the guard room, fast asleep, the guards stood drawn up in line. Indeed, in every room that he entered he found men and women, some standing, some sitting, often with smiling lips but always with closed eyes.

On he went and on to the very heart of the palace, where, in a beautiful room of gold, he saw the loveliest sight in the world—a sleeping princess, a statue in rose and silver, so fair she seemed an angel. He fell on his knees beside her, and looked at her in awe.

Just at that moment the enchantment came to an end. The Princess opened her eyes and saw her dream before her. She smiled on the kneeling youth and said:

"Is it you, my Prince? I have waited long."

They talked for hours, and still had not said half that was in their hearts to say. Meanwhile, everything in the palace waked with the Princess, and everyone took up his task just where he had left it. At nightfall a lady in waiting courtesied to the Princess and announced that supper was served. And after supper the King's son led his bride, in her gorgeous robes of a hundred years ago, to the royal chapel, where they were married by the very priest who had married the father and mother of the Princess.

The next morning the bridegroom and bride left the palace and passed through the dark, gloomy wood into the bright sunshine of the world beyond. And when the Princess turned to look at the castle where she had slept so many years, behold, castle and wood had vanished, and they stood on an open plain.

So the Princess rode with her Prince to his father's court, and there they lived ever after a life as happy as her dream.

CINDERELLA AND HER GODMOTHER

CINDERELLA OR THE LITTLE GLASS SLIPPER

Once upon a time there was a little girl whose dear mother died, and whose father married for his second wife the proudest and unkindest woman that ever was seen. She had two daughters who were exactly like her in every way. The little girl, on the other hand, was all sweetness and goodness, for she took after her mother, who had been the best woman in the world.

No sooner was the wedding over than the new wife began to show her bad temper. She could not bear the gentleness of the little girl because it made the sharp voices and selfish ways of her own daughters seem more hateful, and she put her to doing the hardest work in the house. She made her wash the dishes and scrub the stairs and clean up the rooms till the house was neat enough for the Queen of the Cats, but still the child, at the end of her day's toil, had only a scolding for supper.

At night the poor little girl slept alone on a straw sack in the attic, while her sisters slept in fine rooms on soft beds of the very latest fashion, and had looking glasses so tall that they could see themselves from top to toe. But she bore it all cheerfully, never complaining to her father, who had troubles enough of his own.

When her work was done she used to cuddle down in the chimney corner in the ashes and cinders to keep warm. For this reason she was called Ash-girl; but the younger sister, who was not quite so rude as the elder, called her Cinderella. Now in spite of Cinderella's ragged clothes, she was a hundred times prettier than her sisters in their elegant dresses.

It happened one day that the King's son gave a ball and invited to it all the grand folk. Of course Cinderella's sisters were invited, because with their airs and graces they were very fine ladies indeed.

They were wild with delight. They busied themselves choosing what gowns they should wear and deciding what manner of headdress would become them most. But it meant only more work for Cinderella, because it was she who had to iron her sisters' linen and plait their ruffles and flounces. All day long,

the sisters talked of nothing but of how they were going to dress.

"I," said the elder, "shall wear my red velvet robe, with my wonderful lace trimming."

"I," said the younger, "shall wear my ordinary dropskirt, but I shall drape over it my gold-brocaded train; and I shall put on my emeralds. I shall not look plain, I can tell you that!"

At last they called in Cinderella to ask her advice, for they knew she had the best of taste. She offered to dress their hair for them, and they were glad enough to have her do it.

While she was dressing their hair they said to her:

"Cinderella, don't you wish you might go to the ball?"

"You are only making fun of me," said poor Cinderella. "Ash-girls don't go to balls at the palace, as you very well know."

"Right you are!" they exclaimed. "How people would laugh to see a sooty ash-girl at the ball!"

Any one but Cinderella would have put their hair up all crooked, but Cinderella, who was as good as she was pretty, only tried to make her sisters look as well as she possibly could. They had gone almost two days without eating, so excited were they about going to the ball, but in spite of that, they broke about a dozen corset strings trying to make themselves look slender, and they spent hours and hours before their tall mirrors.

At last the happy evening arrived. The two sisters set out for the ball, and Cinderella watched them as far as her eyes could see. When their carriage had rolled out of sight, she burst into tears. Suddenly her god-mother, a little old lady leaning on an ivory staff, stood before her and asked what the trouble was.

"I want—I want," sobbed poor Cinderella, but the tears came so fast she could say nothing more.

Her godmother, who was a fairy, knew quite well what she wanted. "You wish you might go to the ball. Is it not so?"

"Yes," said Cinderella, with a deep sigh.

"Well, then," said her godmother, "be a good girl and I will see that you go to the ball. Run out into the garden and bring me a pumpkin."

Cinderella did not see what on earth a pumpkin could have to do with her going to the ball, but she ran quickly, chose the biggest and finest pumpkin on the vines, and carried it to her godmother.

Her godmother scooped it out so that nothing but the rind was left. She touched it lightly with her ivory staff, and the pumpkin was changed into a splendid gilded coach.

Then she went and looked into the mouse trap, where she found six live mice. She told Cinderella to lift the door of the trap just a little, and as each mouse ran out she tapped it lightly with her staff, and at once it became a spirited steed. Altogether, they soon had a fine turnout of six prancing mouse-gray horses in bright, jingling harness.

But what to do for a coachman?

"I will go and see if there are not some rats in the rat trap," cried Cinderella. "We might make a coachman out of one of them!"

"Good!" said her godmother. "Run and see."

So Cinderella brought the rat trap. In it there were three big rats. The fairy chose the plumpest one with the longest whiskers, and changed him into a jolly fat coachman with the finest sweeping mustaches you ever saw.

Then the godmother said:

"Go into the garden and bring me the six lizards you will find behind the watering pot."

Cinderella had no sooner brought the lizards than her godmother changed them into six footmen. They jumped up behind the coach and sat there as stiff and straight in their gold-braided uniforms as if

they had done nothing else all their lives. Then the fairy said:

"Now you have all you need to take you to the ball. Are you not happy?"

"Yes," faltered Cinderella, "but how can I go in these ragged clothes?"

The godmother just touched her with her staff, which was really a fairy wand, and in a moment the rags were changed to a dress of gold and silver tissue embroidered with precious stones. And on Cinderella's feet was a pair of glass slippers, the most dainty and graceful little slippers in this world.

Cinderella climbed into her gilded coach, the chubby coachman cracked his whip, but before the fiery horses had sprung forward, her godmother said to her:

"Remember, my child, you must not stay one minute after midnight. For if you do, your coach will change back to a pumpkin, your horses will be mice, your coachman a rat, your footmen lizards, and your beautiful gown the same old clothes you wore before."

Cinderella promised that she would surely leave the ball before midnight, and away she drove, almost beside herself with joy. The King's son, when he heard that a beautiful Princess whom no one knew, had come, ran down the steps to meet her. He gave her his hand as she alighted from the carriage, and led her into the ballroom.

At once everyone became silent. The dancing stopped; the musicians left off playing. No one could do anything but look at this radiant Princess whom no one knew. On all sides was heard the whisper:

"Oh, how beautiful she is!"

Even the old King could do nothing but gaze at her, and he whispered very low to the Queen:

"My dear, not since you were a young girl have I seen any one so charming!"

All the ladies of the court were busy staring at Cinderella's robe, hoping they might be able to copy it the very next day. But where

could they find such glorious stuff, and where could they find sewing women clever enough to follow so rare a pattern?

The young Prince led Cinderella to the seat of honor, and begged for the next dance. She danced so gracefully that everyone admired her more than ever. When supper was served, the young Prince ate nothing, because he could not take his eyes off Cinderella, who seated herself near her sisters and shared with them the fruit and sweetmeats which the Prince gave her. They were very much surprised at such kindness from this great and gracious

lady. As she was still talking with them the clock struck three quarters after eleven, and Cinderella at once excused herself, courtesied to the Prince, and hurried away.

As soon as she reached home she ran to find her godmother and thanked her again and again.

"And, oh, godmother," she coaxed, "may I not go once more tomorrow night? Because the King's son begged me to come."

But before her godmother could make reply her sisters knocked at the door. The fairy godmother disappeared and Cinderella ran to let them in.

"Oh, how long you have been!" cried Cinderella, rubbing her eyes and yawning as if she had just waked.

If Cinderella was sleepy now, you may be sure she had been far from sleepy all the evening!

"If you had been at the ball," said one of her sisters, "you would not have been yawning! There was the most beautiful and the most gracious Princess there that has ever been seen! She showed us a thousand attentions. She shared with us the fruit and sweetmeats which the King's son bestowed upon her."

Cinderella could scarcely conceal her mirth as she asked the name of the Princess.

"We don't know," said her sisters. "The King's son himself would give anything in the world to find out who she is."

Cinderella sighed and said:

"She surely must have been lovely! Oh, how lucky you were to see her! How I wish I could see her, too! Oh, my Lady Javotte, please lend me that yellow frock you wear every day, so that I may go to the ball and look on the Princess!"

"I see myself doing it!" sneered Lady Javotte. "Wouldn't I be silly to lend my nice frock to a dirty little ash-girl!"

Cinderella did not mind, for she would not have known what to do with the yellow dress if Lady Javotte had really lent it to her.

The next night the sisters went to the ball. Cinderella went, too, but she was clad even more charmingly than on the night before. The Prince stayed close beside her, and never stopped whispering love words into her ear. Cinderella was so happy she quite forgot what her godmother had told her. When the first stroke of midnight sounded, she was sure it could not be later than eleven. But when she found it was really twelve, she sprang up and ran out of the ballroom like a startled deer.

The Prince hurried after her, but he could not overtake those flying feet. As she ran, Cinderella dropped one of her glass slippers, and this the prince picked up most carefully.

Cinderella reached home all out of breath, without coach, without footmen, in the same sooty, ragged clothes she wore every day. All she had left of her finery was one little glass slipper.

The Prince asked the guards at the palace door if they had not

seen the Princess run out. No, the guards said, they had seen only a young girl, poorly dressed, and more like a peasant than a princess.

When the two sisters returned from the ball Cinderella asked if the beautiful lady had been there.

"Yes," they said. "But as the clock struck twelve she ran away so fast that she dropped one of her little glass slippers. The King's son found it, and all the rest of the evening he did nothing but look at it. It is plain to be seen he is much in love with its owner, and will never rest until he has found the Princess to whom it belongs."

What they said was true. A few days later the Prince's messenger rode through the streets and blew a great blast on his long silver trumpet. Then he cried in

a loud voice that the King's son would marry the maiden who could wear the glass slipper.

The slipper was tried first on the princesses, then on the duchesses and court ladies, but it fitted no one. Finally it was carried to Cinderella's home, and tried on the two sisters. Each did her best to squeeze her foot into it, but it was far too small.

Cinderella, who had been watching them, and who knew her slipper, said with a smile:

"What if I were to try?"

Her sisters began to jeer at her, but the King's herald turned and looked at her closely. He saw even through the soot that she was beautiful, and declared it was only right that she, too, should try on the slipper. She sat down, he knelt and held the little slipper to her foot, and it fitted her like wax.

The sisters gasped with amazement, but they were even more surprised when Cinderella took the other slipper from her pocket and slipped it on her other foot. No sooner had she done this than her godmother appeared. She touched Cinderella with her wand, and there stood the Princess who had gone to the ball, but even more richly dressed than before. When the two sisters saw that it was really Cinderella who stood before them, they fell on their knees and begged her to forgive them. She lifted them up, kissed them, forgave them, and begged them to love her always.

She was led to the Prince, who thought her lovelier than ever, and married her as soon as the priest could find the wedding service in the prayer book. And then because Cinderella was as good as she was pretty, she took her sisters with her to the palace, and there, after their tempers and manners had improved, she married them to two fine gentlemen of the court.

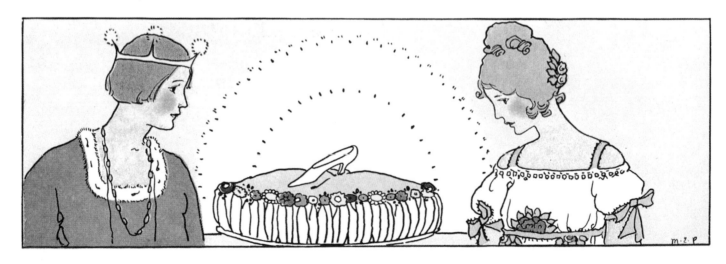

TOADS AND DIAMONDS

Once upon a time there was a widow who had two daughters. The elder was just like her mother in face and in disposition, and both were so disobliging and so rude that there was no living with them. The younger took after her father, who had been the kindest, sweetest-tempered of men, and she was, besides, one of the most beautiful girls that the sun ever looked upon.

As people naturally love those in whom they see themselves, this mother was foolishly fond of her elder daughter and almost hated the younger. She made her eat in the kitchen and work from daylight till dark.

Among other tasks the child had to go twice a day to a spring over a mile and a half from the house and bring home a heavy clay pitcher full of water.

One morning as she stood resting a minute by the fountain, an old woman hobbled up to her. "Please, my bonny lass," she begged, "give me a drink."

"Oh, yes, with all my heart, Goody," said the kind little girl. Then she rinsed out her pitcher, caught the clear, cool water just as it came bubbling from the rock, and held up the pitcher that the old woman might drink more easily.

Refreshed by the sweet water, the beggar leaned on her staff and said to the child: "You are so kind to an old woman, my dear, and so good and so mannerly, that I have a gift for you." For this was a fairy, who had taken the form of a shabby old cripple to see whether this pretty girl was as sweet as she looked. "This shall be the gift," went on the fairy: "At every word you speak there shall come out of your mouth a flower or a jewel."

When the girl reached home, her mother scolded her for staying so long at the fountain. "Please forgive me, dear mother," pleaded the child. And as she spoke there fell from her lips two blush roses, two lovely pearls, and one big, sparkling diamond.

"What is this? What is this?" cried the mother, treading on the roses in her eagerness to pick up the gems. "Am I bewitched or did I really see these pearls and this diamond fall from your mouth? What does it mean, my child?" This was the first time she had ever spoken to her younger daughter so tenderly.

The girl told her all that had happened, and at every word a ruby, an emerald, a sapphire, or a beautiful flower fell from her lips

"As I live," cried the mother, "I must send my other daughter to the fountain. See, my precious, what comes out of your sister's mouth when she speaks. Would you not like, my pet, to have the same wonderful gift given to you? You need only go to the fountain, and when a poor old woman asks you for a drink, give it to her very politely."

"Do I look like a servant?" cried the rude girl. "Is it fit for

me to carry a heavy pitcher to the spring for water?"

"Indeed and you shall go, you minx," snapped her mother, "and go this instant."

Angrily the girl snatched up the best silver pitcher, her mother's wedding pitcher that never went to the well, and set forth grumbling and muttering.

As she stood by the fountain she saw coming out of the woods a lady in a dress that seemed woven out of rainbows. This was the same fairy who had been so generous to the younger sister, but of course Miss Cross-Patch, waiting impatiently for a poor old woman, did not know that.

"Will you give me a drink, my dear?" asked the lady.

"And why should *I* draw water for *you?*" was the saucy answer. "Here is the pitcher, you may stoop down and dip up water for yourself."

"Are these your best manners?" asked the fairy as gently as before. "This, then, must be your gift, since you are so rude and so unkind: At every word you speak there shall drop out of your mouth a snake or a toad."

As soon as the mother saw her favorite coming, she held out her hands to catch the jewels, crying: "Speak, daughter! Speak!"

"Speak what?" answered the girl pettishly. And with the words there dropped from her mouth a toad and a viper.

"Mercy on us!" gasped the mother. "What horrors have we here? You wretch," she screamed, turning to the younger sister, "you are the cause of this, and you shall pay for it, you shall, you shall!" She rushed in fury at the child, who slipped through the door, fled away, and hid in the forest.

That evening the King's son, riding through the woods, heard sobbing and found her crying in a hawthorn thicket. "My pretty maid," he said, leaning from his saddle, "why are you here alone when night is coming on?"

"Oh, sir," replied the girl, "my mother has turned me out of doors."

The Prince was amazed when he saw five pearls and diamonds fall shining from her mouth. "What does this mean?" he cried. "Tell me all that has happened."

So with all manner of flowers and jewels slipping from her lips as she talked, she told him the whole story, and he fell in love with her while she was telling it.

"To be sure," he said to himself, "my father meant me to wed a king's daughter, but such a rain of precious stones is greater treasure than the marriage portion I should receive with any princess, however wealthy." So the King's son led the maiden to the royal palace and there they were married amid great rejoicing.

As for her sister, she was so hateful that her own mother turned her off, and the miserable girl, having wandered about a good while without finding any one to take her in, went to a corner in the wood and there lived as queen of the toads and vipers.

THE FROG PRINCE

One evening a beautiful young princess went into a wood near her father's palace and sat down under an oak tree beside a spring of cool, clear water. She brought with her a golden ball, which was her favorite plaything, and she amused herself by tossing it up and catching it again as it fell. But one time she threw it so high that when the ball came down she could not catch it. It fell on a slope and rolled along until at last it slipped into the spring. The Princess jumped up and looked into the spring for the ball, but the water was very deep—so deep and dark she could not see the bottom. Then she began to weep and sobbed,

"Oh! Oh! if I could only get my gold ball again, I would give all my fine clothes and my pearls and diamonds—everything I have in the world!"

Just as she said this, a big green frog stuck its head out of the spring and asked: "Beautiful Princess, why do you weep?"

"Alas!" said the Princess, "what good can it do to tell you, you old waddler? You cannot help me. My golden ball has fallen into the spring."

"I do not want your pearls and diamonds and fine clothes," croaked the frog, "but if you will love me and let me live with you in the palace and eat from your little gold plate and sleep on your little white pillow, I will bring you your ball again."

"What a silly frog!" thought the Princess. "He is as foolish as he is ugly. He can never climb out of the spring and up the steps of the palace. But perhaps he can get my ball again, so I had better promise him whatever he wants." Then she said to the frog: "If you will bring me my ball from the spring, I promise to do everything you ask."

Without a splash the frog dived deep into the spring. The Princess was still staring at the place where he sank, when he popped his green head out of the water and, sure enough, the ball was in his mouth. He tossed it out on the ground and the young Princess ran to pick it up. She was so happy to have it in her hand again that she never

gave one thought to the frog, but ran home as fast as she could. The frog called after her in his hoarse voice: "Wait, wait, Princess. Take me with you, do!" But the Princess did not stop to say a word— not even "thank you."

Next day, just as the Princess sat down to dinner, she heard a strange noise, flop, flop, flop, slowly coming up the marble staircase. Soon after there came a thump low down at the door, and a hoarse voice said:

"Beautiful Princess, open your door,
  That I may come in and go out no
    more.
  Have you forgotten the vows you
    made
  By the woodland spring, in the oak
    tree's shade?"

The Princess jumped down from her chair and ran and opened the door, and there at her feet sat the frog! She had forgotten all about him and was dreadfully frightened when she saw his fat green body and his wide mouth that was trying

The King said kindly but very firmly to his daughter: "Princesses never break their word. You have made a promise and now you must keep it. Run and let him in."

So the Princess opened the door, and the frog came hop, hop, hopping into the room and up to her chair.

"Pick me up and put me on the table at your side," said he to the Princess, and the Princess dared not refuse. When he had settled himself on the table, the frog said: "Push your gold plate closer to me, that I too may eat out of it." The Princess shuddered but she pushed her plate closer, refusing to eat any more from it herself. When the frog had finished dinner, he said: "I am tired and sleepy; it is far from the well to the palace and the steps are steep. Carry me upstairs and put me on your little white pillow."

And the Princess, hating to touch the clammy creature, took him up between her thumb and finger and carried him upstairs. There she laid him on the pillow of her little bed, but when she laid her own head on the pillow, and the cold frog tumbled against her cheek, her patience left her and she flung him with all her might against the wall.

When he fell down, there was no frog at all, but a handsome young

to smile. Shutting the door in his face, she came back to her seat.

"Who was it, daughter?" asked the King. "What has frightened you?"

"There is an ugly frog at the door," said she, "and he wants to come in. Last night I dropped my golden ball in the spring, and he dived down and brought it out for me. I promised him that he might live with me here and be my playmate, but I felt sure that he could never, never get out of the spring. And now he is at the door and I am afraid!"

Just then there came another thump, and the frog croaked:

"Beautiful Princess, open your door,
  That I may come in and go out no
    more.
  Have you forgotten the vows you
    made
  By the woodland spring, in the oak
    tree's shade?"

when they looked out into the moonlight there was a crystal carriage drawn by eight white horses decked with plumes of snowy feathers and with silver harness. And on the carriage was the Prince's coachman, who had bewailed the loss of his master so long and so bitterly that his heart had well-nigh burst. He had had to put three strong iron bands about it, lest it should break from grief and pain, but as they all set out merrily for the Prince's kingdom, crack, crack, crack went the iron bands, for the heart of the coachman, swelling with joy, had snapped them one after another.

prince stood beside her bed, looking at her with the most grateful eyes that ever were seen.

"Who are you? And where is the frog?" cried the Princess.

"An angry witch changed me to a frog," said the Prince, "and doomed me to remain a frog until some princess should let me eat from her plate and rest on her pillow. This wicked spell," he went on, "you have broken. And now will you marry me and go with me to my father's kingdom? I will love you and be good to you as long as I live."

The Princess, you may be sure, said yes without stopping long to think it over. Just then they heard a prancing in the courtyard, and

DRAKESTAIL

Drakestail was a tiny little fellow. That is why he was given his name of Drakestail. But he had brains enough to fill a big, big head, and he made his brains work for him so hard that before he was very old he had saved a hundred round silver dollars.

Now the King of the country never saved anything, but spent his own money and everybody else's that he could lay his hands on. He heard that Drakestail had money, and rode in his own chariot to borrow it. And you may be sure that Drakestail bragged more than once that he had lent money to the King.

But a year went by, and a year and a day, and the King had not paid back the money nor even a cent of interest; so Drakestail began to feel it was not a good investment. He was a brave little duck, as brave as he was clever, and he finally made up his mind to call on the King and ask for the return of his round silver dollars.

So one fine spring morning, in his best suit of glossy green feathers, Drakestail started for the King's castle, chanting in his flat voice, "Quack, quack, quack! when shall I get my money back?"

He had not gone far when he met
Slyboots, the Fox, prowling about to
see what he could find.

"Good morrow, Neighbor Drakestail," said the Fox. "And whither
away so bright and gay?"

"I am going to the King to get
my money back."

"And may I go with you to the
King?"

"One can't have too many friends,"
said Drakestail to himself. To the
Fox he said: "You may go, but four
legs tire sooner than two legs. Make
yourself quite small, slip down my
throat and into my gizzard, and I will
carry you."

"Clever Drakestail!" chuckled
Slyboots, the Fox. And bag and

baggage he popped into Drakestail's
broad yellow bill and was gone like
a letter into a post box.

Again Drakestail set off, fresh as a
spring breeze, still chanting his funny
song. "Quack, quack, quack! when
shall I get my money back?"

He had not gone far when he met
Lady Leaning Ladder with her feet
on the ground and her head leaning
against the wall.

"Good morrow, Duckie Drakestail," said Lady Leaning Ladder.
"And whither bound, so plump and
round?"

"I am going to the King to get
my money back."

"And may I go with you to the
King?"

"One really can't have too many
friends," said Drakestail to himself.
To Lady Leaning Ladder he said:
"You may go, but wooden feet tire
sooner than web feet. Make yourself
quite small, slip down my throat
and into my gizzard, and I will
carry you."

"Wise Drakestail!" creaked Lady
Leaning Ladder. And as nimble as
though she had joints she was into
his bill and down his throat to keep
company with Friend Fox.

With a "Quack, quack, quack,"
Drakestail set off again, chanting
more cheerily than ever. A little
farther on he met his sweetheart,

Rippling River, wandering quietly along through shade and sunshine.

"Welcome, welcome!" murmered Rippling River.

"Will you play at waterfalling?
Will you paddle a leaf canoe?

Or is something calling, calling,
Calling down the road to you?"

"I am going to the King to get my money back."

"And may I go with you to the King?"

"One really can't have too many friends," said Drakestail to himself. To Rippling River he said: "You may go, but silver sandals tire sooner than these brave red shoes of mine. Slip down my throat and into my gizzard and I will carry you."

"Wonderful Drakestail!" crooned Rippling River. And with all her rushes and lilies she slipped glug, glug, glug, into the yellow bill and down the narrow way and took her place between Friend Fox and Lady Leaning Ladder.

"Quack! Quack!" Drakestail once more was on the road. Just around the turn he met Buzzy Wasp's-nest, drilling his wasps in squads and battalions.

"Greetings, Friend Drakestail!" said Buzzy Wasp's-nest. "Whither and why, so spruce and so spry?"

"I am going to the King to get my money back."

"And may I go with you to the King?"

"One can't have too many friends," said Drakestail to himself. To Buzzy Wasp's-nest he said: "You may, but gauze wings tire sooner than these firm legs of mine. Make yourself quite small, slip down my throat and into my gizzard, and I will carry you."

"Marvelous Drakestail!" hummed Buzzy Wasp's-nest.

And to the rear, marching, he led his rank and file to join the others. Quarters were a little crowded now, but they didn't mind squeezing.

And Drakestail set off again — "quack, quack, quack!"

And now here is the capital and here is Quality Street, and who is it

waddling up the sidewalk, quacking all the way,—who but Drakestail? Hopping up the steps of the King's palace he goes, chanting: "Quack, quack, quack! when shall I get my money back?"

"Rap! Rap!" That is the brass knocker which Drakestail handles none too gently.

"Who is there?" That is the porter, his head thrust out of the little side gate he calls the wicket.

"'T is I, Drakestail. I must speak to the King."

"Speak to the King! Speak to the King! More easily said than done. The King is now dining off pease-pudding and plums, and will not be disturbed."

"Tell him that it is I, and I have come he well knows why."

Bang goes the wicket, and away goes the porter to speak to the King.

Now the King had just sat down to dinner with all his ministers, and the royal chamberlain was tying a napkin around the King's neck.

"Good!" said the King, when the porter told his story. "I know who it is. Let him come in, and turn him into the barnyard with the other fowl."

Down comes the porter and opens the gate.

"Have the grace to enter."

"Good!" says Drakestail to himself. "I shall now see how they eat pease-pudding at court."

"This way, this way," said the porter. "This is the way they go who wish to see the King. And here you are, sir!"

"But this—this is the poultry yard!" You may imagine that Drakestail was in a rage.

"They will, will they?" said he. "But I'll never stop here; the King shall see me, that he shall. Quack, quack, quack, when shall I get my money back?"

Now chickens like chickens, and turkeys like turkeys, and geese like geese, but Drakestail was not turkey nor chicken nor goose, and they began to make fun of his tiny body no bigger than a duck's tail.

"Who is this absurd little creature?" they asked. "And why is he not happy here in the royal poultry yard? Let's peck him to death."

And they rushed at him, cackling and gobbling and hissing in a truly awful fashion.

"Good-by, Drakestail!" said Drakestail to himself. But just then Friend Fox popped into his mind, and he cried:

"Slyboots, Slyboots, come out of
    my gizzard,
  Or Drakestail will die in this
    barnyard blizzard."

Then Slyboots, the Fox, sprang out, rushed at the astonished chickens, geese, and turkeys and sent them all scurrying under the royal barn. Not one remained in sight. And Drakestail, his worries over, began to chant at the top of his voice: "Quack, quack, quack! when shall I get my money back?"

When the King, who was still at table, heard this saucy song and when the poultry keeper told him how his chickens, geese, and turkeys had been driven under the barn, he turned red in the face with wrath.

"Throw this tail of a drake into the well, and make an end of him," he cried.

The servants rushed to carry out his command, as kings' servants always do. In the well Drakestail swam round and round and thought it over. He wasn't afraid of drowning, but he saw no way of getting out of such a deep hole. But wait! There was Lady Leaning Ladder.

"Ladder, Ladder, come out of
    my gizzard.
  Can a duck climb a slippery wall
    like a lizard?"

Leaning Ladder hastened out and placed her two arms on the edge of the well. Then Drakestail waddled up as best he could, and with a flurry of feathers landed in the yard, and

began to chant louder than ever: "Quack, quack, quack! when shall I get my money back?"

When the King, who was still at table and laughing heartily at the joke he had played on Drakestail, heard him still singing about his money, he turned white in the face with rage.

"Heat a furnace," he cried, "and throw this tail of a drake into it. Is he a wizard that he plays such tricks?"

The furnace was soon red hot and the servants seized the duck to throw him into it. But this time Drakestail was not afraid. He counted on his sweetheart, Rippling River.

> "River, River, come out of my
> gizzard.
> With you to help me, I'll play
> the wizard."

Rippling River came flowing forth, and sizz-z-z, fizz-z-z — the furnace fire

was out. Then she flooded the hall of the palace to the height of more than four feet.

And Drakestail, free from his worry, swam on her breast, chanting at the top of his voice: "Quack, quack, quack! when shall I get my money back?"

The King was still at table and thought himself well rid of Drakestail, but when he heard that song and knew that even a fiery furnace could not harm Drakestail, he sprang up from the table brandishing the carving knife.

"Bring him here and I'll cut his throat! Bring him here quick!" cried he.

And two footmen ran to fetch Drakestail.

"At last," said Drakestail proudly, as he hopped up the great stairs, "the King has decided to receive me."

But he almost died of fright when he waddled into the room and saw the King, purple with anger, standing with knife in hand. And all the ministers had their knives in their hands. "It is the end," thought Drakestail. Just then he remembered that he had one friend left, and he cried feebly:

> "Wasp's-nest, Wasp's-nest, come out of
> my gizzard.
> Come quick, before my throat is
> scissored!"

And then! "B-z-z-z! B-z-z-z! At them, boys! At them!" Buzzy Wasp's-nest rushed out with all his wasps. The wasps buzzed about the heads of the King and his ministers, and stung them so fiercely that they were quite beside themselves. Not knowing where to hide, they jumped helter-skelter from the window and broke their necks on the courtyard pavement.

And there stood Drakestail, his four loyal friends about him, in the big dining hall!

And his song changed. "Quack, quack, quack!" he chanted. "Now I shall get my money back." He hunted and he hunted and he hunted in all the drawers and all the cupboards and all the closets, but not one cent could he find. His hundred round silver dollars had been spent—all spent.

As he waddled from room to room he came at last to the great hall where the throne stood. He was tired and hopped up on the throne to think. Meanwhile the people had found their King and his ministers quite, quite dead in the courtyard, and they came rushing into the palace to see what had happened. Through the palace they poured and at length they came to the throne-room. And there on the throne sat Drakestail! You may imagine that

he was surprised when he heard them shout:

"The King is dead, long live the King!
Heaven has sent us down this thing."

By the time the shouting had died away, Drakestail was over his surprise and bowed majestically to the people, just like a real king. There were some who grumbled that they did not want a Drakestail to rule over them, but those who knew Drakestail said he would make a far better king than the spendthrift who lay dead below. So they took the crown off the fallen King's head and set it on Drakestail's head, and it fitted him like wax.

And so Drakestail became king.

The crowning over, he said, "Let's go to supper, Rippling River, Lady Leaning Ladder, Buzzy Wasp's-nest, Friend Fox, and all. I'm so hungry!"

LITTLE RED RIDING HOOD AND THE WOLF

LITTLE RED RIDING-HOOD

Once upon a time there was a little village girl who was as sweet as sugar and as good as bread. Her mother loved her very much, and her grandmother was even fonder of her. This kind grandmother had made her a pretty red cloak with a hood, in which the child looked so bright and gay that everyone called her Little Red Riding-Hood.

One day her mother made some cakes, and said to her: "Go, my child, and see how your grandmother is. I hear she has been ill. Take her one of these cakes and this little pot of butter."

So Little Red Riding-Hood set out at once to see her grandmother, who lived in another village.

As she walked through the woods she met a big wolf. He would have gobbled her up then and there, but some woodcutters were near by and he did not dare. But he did ask her where she was going. The little girl did not know it was dangerous to talk to a wolf, and so she said: "I am going to my grandmother with this cake and little pot of butter."

"Does she live far off?" asked the wolf.

"Oh, yes," answered Little Red Riding-Hood. "She lives beyond the mill you see way down there, at the first house in the village."

"All right," said the wolf. "I'll go and visit her too. I will take this way, and you take that way, and we'll see who gets there first."

And the wolf began to run as fast as he could along the shortest path, while Little Red Riding-Hood kept to the high road. She amused herself as she went along gathering nuts, chasing late butterflies, and making nosegays of the little autumn flowers.

Soon the wolf arrived at the grandmother's cottage, and knocked at the door — tap! tap!

"Who is there?"

"It is your own Little Red Riding-Hood," said the wolf, making his voice sound as much like Little Red Riding-Hood's as he could. "I have brought you a cake and a little pot of butter which mother has sent you."

The good old woman, who wasn't well and so was in bed, called out: "Pull the string, my dear, and the latch will fly up."

The wolf pulled the string and the door opened. He sprang upon the poor old grandmother and swallowed her all in one gulp, for it was more than three days since he had had a bite. He did not feel very well after that, but he shut the door, put on the grandmother's cap, and stretched himself out in the bed to wait for Little Red Riding-Hood. By-and-by Red Riding-Hood came knocking at the door—tap! tap!

"Who is there?"

At first Little Red Riding-Hood was frightened at the hoarse voice of the wolf. But she made up her mind her grandmother must have a cold.

"It is your own Little Red Riding-Hood," she answered. I have brought you a cake and a little pot of butter which mother has sent you."

Then the wolf called out, softening his voice as well as he could: "Pull the string, my dear, and the latch will fly up."

Little Red Riding-Hood pulled the string and the door opened.

When the wolf saw her come in, he hid under the bedclothes and said:

"Put the cake and the little pot of butter on the shelf, and come to bed with me."

And so Little Red Riding-Hood climbed into bed. She was very much surprised to see how strange her grandmother looked in her nightclothes and said:

"Grandmother, what great arms you have!" she cried.

"The better to hug you, my child!"

"Grandmother, what great ears you have!"

"The better to hear you, my child!"

"Grandmother, what great eyes you have!"

"The better to see you, my child!"

"Grandmother, what great teeth you have!"

"The better to eat you!"

With these words the wicked wolf fell upon poor Little Red Riding-Hood. And there the story ends. Nobody knows just what happened. Some say that the woodsmen came in just in time to save Little Red Riding-Hood, and when they cut the wolf open, there was grandmother whole and sound.

RUMPEL-STILT-SKIN

Once upon a time there lived a poor miller who had a very beautiful daughter. He was so proud of her beauty and cleverness he boasted the livelong day about her. One day he even dared tell the King his daughter could spin gold out of straw. Now the King loved gold far better than anything else in his kingdom, and when he heard the miller's boast, he commanded the maiden to be brought before him.

She was so beautiful he almost forgot his purpose, but soon he led the maiden to a large room about half full of straw, gave her a spinning wheel and said: "If all this straw is not spun into gold by morning, you shall die." Then he went out, locked the door with a huge key, and left her alone.

The poor girl sat down in a corner of the room and began to cry, for she knew no more than the King himself about spinning straw into gold. All of a sudden the door opened just a crack and a comical little man squeezed in.

"Good day, miller's daughter," he said. "What are you crying about?"

"Ah me!" she sobbed, "I must die on the morrow, for I know not how to spin this straw into gold."

"What will you give me if I do it for you?" asked the little man.

"This necklace I am wearing," replied the maiden.

The little man agreed and, sitting down at the wheel, sent it round right merrily, and presently the heap of straw was gone and the gold all spun. Then he twisted the necklace twice about his waist, stuck his little sword into this new belt of his and strutted away, leaving his cap for her breakfast.

When the King came next morning, he was very much pleased but far from satisfied. The more gold

he had, the more he wanted. So he led the girl to a still larger room two thirds full of straw, and ordered her on peril of her life to spin it all into gold before sunrise. Again she began to cry and again the little man slipped through the crack of the door and said: "What will you give me, miller's daughter, to spin your straw to-night?"

"This ring on my finger," she replied.

So the droll little man set the wheel whirring again, twice as fast as before, and by daylight all was finished. Then he put on the ring as a bracelet, capered for pride and was gone, leaving his jacket for her breakfast.

The King came at dawn and was delighted to see the store of gold, yet his greedy heart was not satisfied. He took the miller's daughter into a vast chamber packed to the ceiling with straw except where the spinning wheel stood, and said: "Let all this straw be spun into gold to-night and you shall be my queen."

As soon as she was alone, in squeezed the queer little man again and said: "And what shall I have this third time for my labor?"

"I have nothing more," sighed she.

"Then you must promise to give me your first child after you become queen," said the little man.

90

THE KING WAS DELIGHTED TO SEE THE STORE OF GOLD

"But what may not happen before then?" thought the maiden, and as she knew no other way out of her trouble, she promised to do what he asked.

That night he sang as he spun and the wheel whirred thrice as fast as before, so that when the sun shone into the chamber, all the straw was gold. The comical little man had to go out by the window, for the King came earlier than ever, thinking not only of the gold but of the beauty of the miller's daughter, whom he made his queen.

At the birth of her first child the Queen was overjoyed. She had

quite forgotten the queer little man, when one day he slipped into her chamber and said: "Where is the child you promised me?"

Then she was in sore distress. In vain she offered him all the treasures of the kingdom. But as the queer little man tucked the royal baby snugly under his arm, she gave such a cry that his odd little heart, like a dry currant, softened and he said: "I will give you three days to guess my name. If you can do it, you may keep the child." And he dropped the baby with a bump back into the cradle.

The Queen lay awake the night long, thinking of all the names she had ever heard. The next day when the little man came, she began with the names of the three kings of the East, Caspar, Melchior, Balthazar, and asked him the names of all the kings and princes that had lived since. But to all of them he gleefully said:

"Ho, ho! No, no, my Royal Dame!
That's not my name; that's not
my name."

The next day she sent messengers throughout the kingdom to collect all the curious names of poor folk. And when the little man skipped in, she began with: "Cow-ribs, Bandy-legs, Spindle-shanks, Snub-nose, Red-top, and so on for five hundred more.

But to all of them the little man shouted:

> "Ho, ho! No, no, my Royal Dame!
> That's not my name; that's not
> my name."

The third day the last of the messengers came back weary and worn from his long journey and said: "Forgive me, sorrowful Queen. I could find no new name but one. Yesterday as I was passing through a strange wood, I saw a tiny, red-roofed hut and in the dooryard there capered a funny little man who sang:

> 'To-day I bake; to-morrow I brew;
> To-day for one; to-morrow for two.
> For how should she learn, poor
>   Royal Dame,
> That Rumpel-stilt-skin is my name?'"

When the Queen heard this, she surprised the messenger by a peal of laughter, for she knew the singer must have been her little gold-spinner. So, when at sunset he came skipping in and said: "Tell me my name if you can," she asked, putting on a doleful look and clasping her baby to her breast: "Is it Hans?"

"No."

"Is it Fritz?"

"No."

"Well then, it's Rumpel-stilt-skin."

"The fairies have told you! The fairies have told you!" shrieked the little man in a rage, and he stamped his right foot so deep down through the floor that he could not pull it out. Becoming more angry still, he laid hold of his left foot with both hands and jerked so hard that he split himself in two, for he was really made of gingerbread, as all Rumpel-stilt-skins are.

"OH, DEAR, DEAR!" SAID THE LITTLE OLD MAN, "ROBBERS MUST HAVE WAYLAID THIS POOR STRANGER"

THE THREE WISHES

In a little house in a woods there once lived a little old man and a little old woman. The little old man was a woodchopper. Every day he cut down big trees in the woods and chopped them into firewood.

When he had cut enough firewood to fill his cart, he would hitch his old gray donkey to his cart and haul the load of wood to town and sell it.

One evening, as he was driving his empty cart from town, he saw a man lying beside the road. The little old man stopped his donkey, and got down from his cart to see what was the matter.

The man beside the road was lying very still. His eyes were closed and there was a big bump on his head where something had hit him.

"Oh, dear, dear!" said the little old man, when he saw that the stranger was hurt. "Robbers must have waylaid this poor stranger."

Just then the man opened his eyes. "What has happened, kind sir," asked the little old man, "that you lie beside the road and have a big bump on your head?"

"Robbers waylaid me," said the stranger. "They took my horse and they took all my money, and then they hit me on the head with a big club and ran away. That is why I lie beside the road and have a big bump on my head, for they hurt me sorely."

"What a dreadful thing!" said the little old man. "But we will soon fix you up and make you well again." And the little old man lifted the hurt stranger into his cart very, very gently, and drove slowly home with him.

When he reached home it was almost dark. The little old woman saw her husband carrying the stranger into the house, and she said, "What have you there, old man?"

"It is a poor stranger who was lying beside the road," replied the little old man. "Robbers waylaid him and took his horse and all his money. Then they hit him with a big club and ran away, and he lay beside the road until I found him, for they hurt him sorely."

"What a dreadful thing!" cried the little old woman. "We must take good care of him, and make him well again." And she bustled about, turning down the covers and making ready their best bed. Soon the poor hurt stranger was lying in the big soft bed instead of beside the hard road.

The little old woman gave him some medicine, and bandaged the big bump on his head, and he fell asleep.

When morning came, and the stranger woke up, he was feeling ever so much better. The little old woman and the little old man were glad to see that he was better, and they gave him a good breakfast. After he had eaten that, the stranger felt better than ever.

THE STRANGER HELD OUT A LITTLE BROWN NUT

"I feel so much better," said he, "that I must put on my clothes and walk about a little."

So he got up and put on his clothes, and he walked about the dooryard. And after he had walked about a little, he felt so well and strong that he said, "I am feeling well and strong again, and I must now continue my journey."

When the little old lady heard him say this, she fixed the stranger a fine lunch to carry with him, and the little old man gave the stranger his best cane to help him over the rough roads.

Their kindness made the stranger very happy, and he said to them, "I thank you kindly, my fine people. But for you, I might still be lying beside the hard road. And so, for your kindness to a poor stranger, I am going to reward you."

"Oh, no, no!" said the little old woman and the little old man. "We did not help you for the sake of any reward."

"Therefore you deserve it all the more," said the stranger, with a smile. "One thing the robbers did not take from me, and so I give it to you," and he held out a little brown nut.

"What a fine little nut!" said the little old man. It looked just like any ordinary nut, but he did not want to hurt the stranger's feelings by saying so.

"Ah, it is a wonderful nut," the stranger said. "It was given to me long ago by a very wise man, and whoever owns it will have his first three wishes fulfilled. But after three wishes are made, the nut will lose its magic power. So think well before you wish," and the stranger gave the little brown nut to the little old man and the little old woman. Then he walked away to continue his journey.

"What a wonderful reward!" exclaimed the little old woman. "Just think, we can make three wishes for anything we like, and have them come true."

"We can become the richest people in the world, and live in a fine palace," said the little old man. "And we can wear new clothes every day."

"But we have always been happy living just as we are," said the little old woman, wisely. "We must be very careful, and wish only for the best, or we may not care for what we get after we get it. So let us think carefully, and choose only the best."

"Very well," said her husband. "Let us put the nut up on the shelf over the fireplace, and this evening, make our wishes."

THE LITTLE OLD WOMAN LOOKED AT THE MAGIC NUT

So the little old man and the little old woman put the little brown nut up on the shelf over the fireplace, and set about their work.

And as they worked all through the day, they kept thinking about the three wishes. They thought of many things to wish for, but each time they would think of something that seemed better, and change their minds.

That evening when they sat down to supper they did not eat much for thinking of the three wishes. At last, when the supper dishes were all washed and put away, the little old man and the little old

97

"WE MIGHT WISH FOR A FINE PALACE,"
SAID THE LITTLE OLD MAN

"Goodness! I hardly know what to wish for!" cried the little old man.

"Gracious! I don't either!" cried the little old woman.

So they talked on, and thought of many things they might get with the three wishes, but never a thing could they agree upon.

Presently, it began to get late. The little old man began to feel hungry, for he had eaten very little supper for thinking of the three wishes. So now, being hungry, he stopped thinking about the three wishes and began to think about something to eat.

And then, not noticing what he was doing, and almost before he knew it, he said, "I wish I had a nice pan of sausages!" And in the twinkling of an eye, there was a pan of sausages before him, sizzling on the coals of the fire.

The little old woman was very much surprised. "Why, old man," she cried, "you have used one of the three wishes just to wish for a pan of sausages!"

And the little old man stared in wonder, for so he had!

Then the little old woman began to grow angry. "You wished for sausages, when you might have wished for all the money in the world!" she exclaimed. And then, without thinking and almost before

woman sat down before the fireplace to use their three wishes.

"We might wish for a fine palace and lots of servants to wait upon us," said the little old man.

"And we might wish for much money, so that we should never have to work any more," said the little old woman.

"And we might wish for a fine coach, with eight big white horses to draw it," said the little old man.

"And we might wish for fine clothes and jewels to wear when we ride out to see the world," said the little old woman.

she knew it, she said, "You old fool, I wish your pan of sausages was fastened to your long nose!"

And there, all in the twinkling of an eye, the pan of sausages was fastened to the little old man's long nose! A big brass ring ran right through the middle of his long nose, and from it the pan of sausages hung by a chain.

"Oh! oh!" shouted the little old man. "Now see what you've done! You've used up the second wish just to hang a pan of sausages from my nose!"

And the little old woman stared in wonder, for so she had!

When she saw what she had done she was no longer angry, but sorry.

"Oh, dear, dear!" said she. "What dreadful thing have I done?" and she tenderly lifted the pan of sausages and set it on a stool beside her little old man so that it would not hang so heavily from his long nose.

"Well, anyway," said the little old woman, "we still have one wish left. With it we can surely wish for all the gold and jewels and fine clothes we need to make us rich for the rest of our days."

"Gold, say you? Jewels and fine clothes?" cried the little old man. "What good can they ever do me, if for the rest of my days I must have a big brass ring through

THE PAN OF SAUSAGES HUNG BY A CHAIN FROM THE OLD MAN'S NOSE

my nose and a heavy pan of sausages hanging from it?"

"That is very true," mourned the little old woman, sadder than ever. So she thought the matter over, and thought of what she had done, and felt so sorry that the tears ran down her cheeks. And as for the little old man, he just sat, looking sadly at the pan of sausages hung from his nose, and wondering how he could ever get rid of it.

All at once the little old woman brightened up. "We were never unhappy before, when we had no thought of riches and jewels and fine clothes," she said. "And we can be just as happy again even if we never get them."

"That is very true," said the old man sadly, for the big brass ring was hurting his long nose. "I was much happier before I ever thought of having three wishes, for then I never had a pan of sausages hung from my nose."

"Then we will just wish the pan of sausages off your nose with the third wish," the little old woman cried, "and then we shall be just as happy as we were before!"

"That's the very thing!" exclaimed the little old man. "If we are happy, what reason will there be for us to make wishes?"

So, together, they wished the pan of sausages off the old man's nose. And at once, in the twinkling of an eye, there was the pan of sausages sizzling over the hot coals again. The big brass ring through the little old man's long nose had disappeared entirely, and the chain also.

The little old man rubbed his long nose happily, and then he laughed merrily because he was so glad that the pan of sausages was no longer hanging from it. And the little old woman laughed also, because everything had ended so well.

So the little old woman and the little old man laughed together, long and heartily, and then they ate the sausages that were sizzling in the pan upon the coals. And they lived together happily forever after, contented with what they had. Nor did they ever feel sad because they had got only a pan of sausages with their three wishes.

For, you see, the sausages had tasted wonderfully good to them.

100

THE OLD WOMAN AND HER PIG

One day an old woman was sweeping her house, and as she was sweeping she found a little crooked sixpence.

"Now what shall I buy with this little sixpence?" she said to herself. "I think I will go to market and buy a little pig."

And so, as soon as her work was done, she went to market and bought a fine little white pig. She tied a string to one of piggy's legs so that she could drive him home, and as she was driving him home she came to a stile.

"Please, piggy," she said, "jump over the stile." But the pig would not.

"Oh, dear! Oh, dear!" cried the old woman. "Piggy won't jump over the stile; and I shan't get home tonight!"

So she left the pig by the stile and went on a little farther. As she went along she met a dog, and she said to him, "Dog! dog! bite pig; piggy won't jump over the stile; and I shan't get home tonight!" But the dog would not.

A little farther on she saw a stick, and she said to it, "Stick! beat dog; dog won't bite pig; piggy won't jump over the stile; and I shan't get home tonight!" But the stick would not.

Soon she saw a fire, and she said to it, "Fire! fire! burn stick; stick won't beat dog; dog won't bite pig; piggy won't jump over the stile; and I shan't get home tonight!" But the fire would not.

Then the old woman saw some water, and she said to it, "Water! water! quench fire; fire won't burn stick; stick won't beat dog; dog won't bite pig; piggy won't jump over the stile; and I shan't get home tonight!" But the water would not.

Then the old woman saw an ox, and she said, "Ox! ox! drink water; water won't quench fire; fire won't burn stick; stick won't beat dog; dog won't bite pig; piggy won't jump over the stile; and I shan't get home tonight!" But the ox would not.

Before long the old woman met a butcher, and she said to him, "Butcher! butcher! kill ox; ox won't drink water; water won't quench fire; fire won't burn stick; stick

"PLEASE, PIGGY," SAID THE OLD WOMAN, "JUMP OVER THE STILE"

won't beat dog; dog won't bite pig; piggy won't jump over the stile; and I shan't get home tonight!" But the butcher would not.

Then the old woman saw a rope, and she said to it, " Rope! rope! hang butcher; butcher won't kill ox; ox won't drink water; water won't quench fire; fire won't burn stick; stick won't beat dog; dog won't bite pig; piggy won't jump over the stile; and I shan't get home tonight!" But the rope would not.

A little farther on, the old woman saw a rat, and she said to it, "Rat! rat! gnaw rope; rope won't hang butcher; butcher won't kill ox; ox won't drink water; water won't quench fire; fire won't burn stick; stick won't beat dog; dog won't bite pig; piggy won't jump over the stile; and I shan't get home tonight!" But the rat would not.

And then the old woman met a cat, and she said to him, "Cat! cat! catch rat; rat won't gnaw rope; rope won't hang butcher; butcher won't kill ox; ox won't drink water; water won't quench fire; fire won't burn stick; stick won't beat dog; dog won't bite pig; piggy won't jump over the stile; and I shan't get home tonight!"

"Yes," said the cat; "if you will go to the cow in the pasture yonder and get a saucer of milk for me, I will catch the rat."

So the old woman went to the cow in the pasture, and said, "Cow! cow! give me a saucer of milk."

"Yes," said the cow; "if you will climb over the fence to that haystack yonder, and bring me an armful of hay, I will give you the milk." So over the fence climbed the old woman, and she brought an armful of hay to the cow.

As soon as the cow had eaten the hay she gave the old woman a saucer of milk, and away the old woman hurried to carry it to the cat.

In a very short time the cat lapped up the milk, and then he washed the last drop of it from his whiskers.

When he had finished washing his whiskers the cat began to catch the rat; the rat began to gnaw the rope; the rope began to hang the butcher; the butcher began to kill the ox; the ox began to drink the water; the water began to quench the fire; the fire began to burn the stick; the stick began to beat the dog; the dog began to bite the pig; and—

The little piggy squealed as loud as he could, and jumped over the stile.

And so the old woman got home that night, after all!

GOING OUT INTO THE WORLD TO SEEK THEIR FORTUNE

HOW JACK FOUND HIS FORTUNE

There was once a bright boy whose name was Jack. Jack was always so kind and friendly that everybody liked him, and wished for him the best of fortune. One morning Jack, who had been hearing of the wonderful things to be seen out in the great world beyond his village, decided to set out and see what he could find.

He hadn't gone far when he saw a cat sitting beside the road, washing its face.

"Where are you going, Jack?" asked the cat.

"I am going out into the world to seek my fortune," answered Jack.

"May I come along with you?" asked the cat.

"Yes," said Jack, glad to have company. "The more, the merrier."

So on they went, Jack and the cat, hippity-hop, hippity-hop! And after a while they came upon a dog, burying a bone beside the road.

"Where are you going, Jack?" asked the dog.

"I am going out into the world to seek my fortune."

"May I come along with you?"

"Yes," said Jack, glad to have company. "The more, the merrier."

So on they went, Jack and the cat and the dog, hippity-hop, hippity-hop, hippity-hop! And after a while they came upon a goat, nibbling the grass beside the road.

"Where are you going, Jack?" asked the goat.

"I am going out into the world to seek my fortune."

"May I come along with you?"

"Yes," said Jack, glad to have company. "The more, the merrier."

So on they went, Jack and the cat and the dog and the goat, hippity-hop, hippity-hippity-hop! And after a while they came upon a bull, standing in the shade of a tree beside the road.

JACK SAW FIERCE ROBBERS COUNTING STOLEN GOLD

"Where are you going, Jack?" asked the bull.

"I am going out into the world to seek my fortune."

"May I come along with you?"

"Yes," said Jack, glad to have company. "The more, the merrier."

So on they went, Jack and the cat and the dog and the goat and the bull, hippity-hop, hippity-hop, hippity-hop! And after a while they came upon a rooster, scratching for worms beside the road.

"Where are you going, Jack?" asked the rooster.

"I am going out into the world to seek my fortune."

"May I come along with you?"

"Yes," said Jack, glad to have company. "The more, the merrier."

So on they went, Jack and the cat and the dog and the goat and the bull and the rooster, hippity-hop, hippity-hop! All going out into the world to seek their fortunes, hippity-hippity-hop!

And they went hippity-hopping along all day, until the sun had almost set and it was getting dark.

All through the day, as they had gone along, the road had grown narrower and narrower, until now it was just a path that led through thick woods.

"We must find a place to sleep tonight," said Jack to his companions. "Perhaps if we go on a little farther we may find a house where we can stay."

So on they went through the dark woods, looking for a house where they might sleep that night.

At last, after they had gone on a little farther, they saw a light in the dark woods. When they came closer, they saw that it was the lighted window of a house.

"Wait here for me," said Jack to his companions, "and I'll ask the people in the house if we may sleep there tonight."

So, leaving the others where they were, Jack went toward the lighted window.

And what did he see, when he looked through the window, but a band of fierce robbers, sitting at a table! They were counting over great heaps of stolen gold that lay before them!

Jack did not dare to let the robbers know that he had seen them, so he crept back to where his companions were waiting for him.

"Perhaps we can frighten them away," he said, after he had told his companions what he had seen.

Quietly, Jack led them nearer the house, and there he whispered to them what each one was to do. When he gave the word, each was to make as much noise as he could, in his own fashion. So when they were ready, Jack gave the word.

And then—oh, my!—what a dreadful uproar began! Jack yelled, and the cat yowled, and the dog howled, and the goat bleated, and the bull bellowed, and the rooster crowed, every one just as loud and as long as he could! All together, they sounded so fearsome that the robbers jumped up in great fright and ran out of the house and away, leaving their gold on the table behind them.

Then Jack and his companions had the house all to themselves. So pleased were they to have a place to sleep that night, and so funny

JACK PUT THE CAT IN A BIG CHAIR

had the robbers looked as they ran away, that they all laughed heartily.

Jack, however, was afraid that the robbers would come back after their gold later, in the middle of the night. So when bedtime came he put the cat in a big chair in front of the fire, and he put the dog under the table. Then he put the goat up at the top of the stairs, and he put the bull down in the cellar, and told the rooster to fly up on the roof. Then Jack went to bed and soon fell sound asleep.

Sure enough, in the middle of the night the chief of the robbers slipped back to the house to get the gold. He left his men waiting for

THE GOAT, WITH HIS HARD HEAD, BUTTED THE ROBBER CHIEF

him in the woods. But it was not very long before he hurried back, and instead of the gold—oh! what a fearsome tale the robber chief brought to them!

"I went to the house," he said, "and went in and tried to sit down in my big chair. But there was a terrible dwarf already sitting in it, and he—oh, my!—he stuck half a dozen daggers into me!"

(That was the cat sticking its claws into him, you know.)

"Then I stepped up to the table to get the gold. But there was a more terrible dwarf under the table, and he—oh, my!—he cut my leg with sharp knives!"

(That was the dog biting him with his sharp teeth, you know.)

"To get away from them both, I ran up the stairs. But there was a man up there waiting for me, and he—oh, my!—he hit me so hard with his club that he knocked me down the stairs again."

(That was the goat butting him with his hard head, you know.)

"So I rushed down into the cellar to get away from them all. But there—oh, dear me!—there was a giant down there with two big sharp swords which he pricked me with, just before he threw me out of the cellar."

(That was the bull touching him with his sharp horns, and tossing him with his head, you know.)

"So I ran out of the house as quickly as I could, and just then I heard the worst one of all! He was a terrible fellow who was sitting up on the roof, and as soon as I came out of the house he started yelling and yelling: 'Cook him in a stew! Cook him in a stew! Cook him in a stew!'"

(And that, you know, was the rooster crying, "Cock-a-doodle-doo!")

"The daggers and knives and clubs and swords were bad enough," said the chief, "but it would be just too awful to be cooked in a stew!"

So the robbers, all very much frightened at the thought of such a dreadful fate, decided that they would leave this dangerous place just as soon as they could, and go far away. As for the gold, the terrible beings in the house could have it if they wanted it. For the robbers certainly weren't going to risk being cooked in a stew just for the sake of a few bags of gold!

When morning came, Jack made sure that the robbers had gone away, and then he divided the gold with his companions.

After that, they all started gayly back home, each with his fortune which had been found so quickly. The cat hung its bag of gold on its tail, the dog had his tied around his neck, the bull and the goat carried theirs on their horns, while Jack had his heavy bag on his shoulders.

And the rooster carried a big gold piece in his beak, which was a good thing, as it kept him from calling all the time:

"Cock-a-doodle-doo!
Cook him in a stew!"

THE ROOSTER CARRIED A GOLD PIECE IN HIS BEAK

THE TEENY-TINY WOMAN - *nana's favorite*

Once upon a time there was a teeny-tiny woman who lived in a teeny-tiny house in a teeny-tiny village. One day this teeny-tiny woman put on her teeny-tiny bonnet and went out of her teeny-tiny house to take a teeny-tiny walk.

And when this teeny-tiny woman had gone a teeny-tiny way, she came to a teeny-tiny gate. She opened the teeny-tiny gate and she walked through it a teeny-tiny way until she found herself in a teeny-tiny woods. And there this teeny-tiny woman saw a teeny-tiny red hen sitting beneath a teeny-tiny tree.

"Oh, if I only had this teeny-tiny hen in my teeny-tiny house!" cried the teeny-tiny woman in her teeny-tiny voice. "Then this teeny-tiny hen could lay a teeny-tiny egg for me every day for my teeny-tiny breakfast!"

So this teeny-tiny woman picked up the teeny-tiny hen from under the teeny-tiny tree, and carried her away in her teeny-tiny arms. She hurried a teeny-tiny bit as she

110

went back through the teeny-tiny gate, and soon she was at home again in her teeny-tiny house.

And when the teeny-tiny woman got home to her teeny-tiny house, she was a teeny-tiny bit tired. So she went up her teeny-tiny stairs to her teeny-tiny bedroom, and there she put the teeny-tiny hen in a teeny-tiny cupboard and shut the teeny-tiny door.

"Now," said the teeny-tiny woman to herself, "while I take a teeny-tiny nap and rest myself a teeny-tiny bit, perhaps the teeny-tiny hen will lay a teeny-tiny egg for me."

And then the teeny-tiny woman lay down on her teeny-tiny bed and pulled the teeny-tiny bedclothes up around her, to take a teeny-tiny nap.

She had been asleep just a teeny-tiny while, when she was awakened by a teeny-tiny voice from the teeny-tiny cupboard, which said:

"GIVE ME MY HEN!"

The teeny-tiny woman was a teeny-tiny bit frightened, so she hid her teeny-tiny head under the teeny-tiny bedclothes and went to sleep again.

And when the teeny-tiny woman had been asleep again for a teeny-tiny while, the teeny-tiny voice again cried out from the teeny-tiny cupboard. And this time it spoke a teeny-tiny bit louder, and said:

"GIVE ME MY HEN!"

This made the teeny-tiny woman a teeny-tiny bit more frightened, so she hid her teeny-tiny head a teeny-tiny bit farther under the teeny-tiny bedclothes, and went to sleep again.

And when this teeny-tiny woman had been asleep again for a teeny-tiny while, the teeny-tiny voice from the teeny-tiny cupboard cried out again, a teeny-tiny bit louder than ever:

"GIVE ME MY HEN!"

And at this, the teeny-tiny woman was a teeny-tiny bit more frightened than she had been before, so she stuck her teeny-tiny head out from under the bedclothes, and she said in her very loudest teeny-tiny voice:

"TAKE IT!"

THE TEENY-TINY WOMAN AND THE TEENY-TINY HEN